CLASS PETS

Fuzzy Fights Back

CLASS PETS

CLASS PETS

PETS

#4: Fuzzy Fights Back

Bruce Hale

Scholastic Inc.

Text and illustrations copyright © 2018 by Bruce Hale

This book is being published simultaneously in hardcover by Scholastic Press.

All rights reserved. Published by Scholastic Inc., *Publishers since 1920*.
SCHOLASTIC, SCHOLASTIC PRESS, and associated logos are trademarks and/or registered trademarks of Scholastic Inc.

The publisher does not have any control over and does not assume any responsibility for author or third-party websites or their content.

ISBN 978-1-338-14527-4

10 9 8 7 6 5 4 3   19 20 21 22 23

Printed in the U.S.A.   40

First printing 2019

Book design by Baily Crawford

To Amy McMillion Goldsmith
and the cool kids of
Daves Avenue School

CONTENTS

CHAPTER 1

The Great Defender

Fuzzy awoke to the sound of clacking. For a moment, he felt disoriented. His sensitive guinea pig nose didn't detect the usual odors of Miss Wills's classroom: glue, dry-erase markers, and sweaty kids.

Where was he?

Blinking the sleep from his eyes, Fuzzy checked out his surroundings. Tan sofa, poofy burgundy armchairs, widescreen TV. *Oh yeah*. He chuckled, nodding to himself. He'd come home for the weekend with Malik Summers, Room 5-B's top student from last week.

With a yawn and a stretch, Fuzzy rose from the footstool he'd been napping on and hopped to the floor. As the clacking continued, angry voices rose in the next room. Fuzzy's ears perked up. It sounded like an argument.

Was Malik in trouble?

All classroom pets took an oath to comfort and protect their students, anywhere, anytime, anyhow. Fuzzy shook himself. No more Nap Rodent. It was time for him to become Action Rodent!

Following the noises, he trotted out of the den and into the Summerses' living room. As he rounded the corner, Fuzzy gasped and stopped short.

The furniture had been pushed back, and in the cleared space, a bigger boy was attacking Malik with a stick! Malik swung his own stick to block it—*clack!*

"How dare you threaten my brother, Spartan dog!" cried Malik. He counterattacked with a *whunk-whunk-whack*. But the taller boy easily fought him off.

Fuzzy frowned. Why was Malik calling the other boy a dog when he was so clearly human? Why were they fighting? He watched, wide-eyed, as the two traded a series of blows.

Click-clack-clunk!

The fight ranged up onto the sofa and back down to the floor.

"Your brother is a stinker!" yelled the bigger boy, his golden hair flopping into his eyes.

"And you're a bigger one!"

"He stole my king's wife, and now he's gonna pay."

"Over my dead body," growled Malik.

Fuzzy looked from one of them to the other, thoroughly mystified. He felt like he'd wandered into the middle of one of those foreign movies Miss Wills watched sometimes. Nothing made sense. Malik didn't have a brother; he had an older sister. And what was all this about stealing wives?

"King Menelaus is a doo-doo head!" cried Malik. "Take that!" He aimed a blow at Floppy Hair's belly.

The taller boy spun aside, whacking Malik on the arm, then the shoulder.

Fuzzy bristled. This overgrown bully was hurting his student. Nobody messed with Room 5-B's kids while Fuzzy was on duty.

No matter how tall, no matter how tough, Floppy Hair was going down!

Snarling, "Leave him alone!" Fuzzy hurled himself straight at the stranger. His eyes were wide. His teeth were bared. Heck, he might even bite the blockhead.

Floppy Hair brandished his stick. "Die, Trojan pond scum!" He chased Malik around the table, and Fuzzy had to gallop extra hard to keep up.

Then he saw his chance. They were coming around again.

Switching directions and rebounding off the sofa, Fuzzy launched himself at the bigger boy's legs. As he flew, he heard Malik shout, "Watch out for Fuzzy!"

The next seconds seemed to unspool in slow motion.

Floppy Hair dodged. Fuzzy sailed past him, tumbling onto the floor.

The boy caught his foot on the table and tripped, stick still raised.

He toppled forward.

Malik turned.

The stick descended, straight at Malik's head.

Fuzzy gasped. "No!"

Ka-tonk!

It struck Malik right between the eyes. With a grunt, the boy crumpled onto the carpet.

Holy haystacks!

Fuzzy's heart caught in his throat. Neither boy moved.

Was Malik . . . ?

Rising onto his hands and knees, Floppy Hair looked over at his fallen enemy. "Dude? Are you okay?"

Guilt wrestled with anger in Fuzzy's gut. On the one hand, if this noodlehead had killed Malik, Fuzzy swore he'd find out how to catch rabies, then bite the bully until he caught it too.

On the other hand, Fuzzy was supposed to protect his students, but his actions led to Malik getting hurt. *Bad class pet.* He crept forward, gaze fixed on Malik.

The boy's eyes were closed. His dark lashes rested on his cheeks. He lay so still.

"What's going on in there?" a woman's voice called from the next room.

Before Fuzzy knew it, Mrs. Summers strode into view. At the sight of her son, the curly-haired woman stiffened. "Malik!" she cried, rushing to his side.

As she kneeled beside him, her son began to stir. Fuzzy let out a long breath. The boy was still alive. He wanted to rush forward and comfort Malik, but the weight of guilt anchored him behind the table leg.

"Careful, don't sit up yet," said Malik's mother. "What happened? Are you all right?" Her hands patted her son all over, searching for an injury.

"It's my fault." Floppy Hair joined them. "I tripped and hit him with my sword."

"You *tripped?*" Mrs. Summers squawked.

The blond boy flinched. "It was an accident. I was trying to avoid the guinea pig, and I caught my foot on the table."

"The *guinea pig?*" Frowning, Malik's mother scanned the room.

"Is Fuzzy okay?" Malik pushed up onto his elbows to see.

"Is *Fuzzy* okay?" his mom echoed.

For some reason, Fuzzy noticed, she kept repeating everything the boys said, only louder and more intensely.

"Yeah," said Malik, rubbing his forehead. "He got all excited because we were rehearsing our scene, and he ran into the middle of things. Where is he?"

"Rehearsing a *scene?*" Now Fuzzy was repeating things. He smacked his own forehead. Of course. The boys weren't trying to kill each other. They were practicing their parts for the fifth-grade play about the Trojan War.

Oops. Fuzzy's ears tingled with embarrassment.

"Don't worry about that rodent," said Malik's mom. She brushed aside her son's hand and probed the reddened area on his forehead. "How does this feel?"

"It's no big de—*ow!*" said Malik. "Just a little sore."

The curly-haired woman bit her lip. "You were out cold."

"Only for a few seconds," said Floppy Hair.

"You're going to the emergency room for a quick check, just to be sure," said Mrs. Summers.

"But I'm fine," said the blond boy.

"Not you, Brayden. Run along home, now; you've done enough."

"I'm fine too," Malik insisted.

Helping her son to his feet, Malik's mother said, "Let's let the doctor decide, okay, lamb chop?"

As blond Brayden waved good-bye and shuffled off, Malik scanned the room. "Where's Fuzzy? Gotta make sure he's okay."

Fuzzy stepped out from behind the table leg, head bowed.

Mrs. Summers scowled. "That creature has caused enough trouble. Put it in its cage and call your teacher."

"But, Mom—"

"Soon as we get back from the ER, she's going to take that thing away for good."

"But Fuzzy's my reward."

Arching an eyebrow, Mrs. Summers said, "Some reward. Real rewards don't endanger students."

"Mom, you've got it all wrong." Malik picked up Fuzzy in the gentle grip—one hand around the chest and one under the hindquarters. "Fuzzy's like our class mascot. The best student each week gets to take him home. It's a tradition."

"Is it?" said Mrs. Summers, her lips a grim line. "Then it's about time for this tradition to change."

CHAPTER 2

In a Cold Threat

Fuzzy spent the next couple of hours in guinea pig jail, feeling as blue as a baby Smurf's tears. Later, when Miss Wills came to pick him up, Fuzzy learned that Malik was indeed just fine. The boy had gotten a little bump on his forehead. No big deal.

Still, that didn't stop Mrs. Summers from scolding Fuzzy's teacher and saying mean things about class pets.

All through Sunday at Miss Wills's house, Fuzzy worried about how his actions with Malik might affect his class. Would the teacher end her tradition of giving top students a weekend with Fuzzy? But when Monday morning came and she made no such announcement, he began to relax.

Probably Mrs. Summers was just blowing off steam. Probably she didn't mean what she said. After all, who didn't like class pets? They were a vital part of student life at Leo Gumpus Elementary, and likely to stay so for many years to come.

By lunchtime, Fuzzy had settled back into his usual routine, convinced that nothing was wrong. He had no idea just how mistaken he was.

As students tromped back into the room after lunch, Gabe hurried over to Abby and whispered something. She frowned, said, "No way!" and murmured the message to Messy Mackenzie. Whatever it was, the word spread around the room at the speed of gossip. The volume rose.

By the time the bell rang, the whole class was humming. "Settle down, please," said the teacher.

Finally, the students quieted. But their gazes remained sharp, expectant.

"Now, when we conduct an experiment using the scientific method," Miss Wills began, "we need to cover certain basic steps. Can anyone—?"

A forest of hands shot into the air.

The teacher smiled. "Such enthusiasm. Yes, Maya?"

"Is it true?" Maya asked.

"The scientific method?" said Miss Wills. "Well, it's a way of determining what's true . . ."

Maya shook her head. "No. Is it true that Principal Flake might take away classroom pets?"

"*What*?!" squeaked Fuzzy, overturning his water bowl.

"What?" said Miss Wills. From the look on the teacher's face, she felt the same way he did. "Where did you hear that?"

"It's all over school," said Gabe. "Is it true?"

"They can't get rid of Fuzzy, can they?" blurted Nervous Lily.

Miss Wills's forehead crinkled. "This is the first I've heard of it. I can't believe that Mrs. Flake would approve something like that."

"But *can* she do it?" Loud Brandon asked.

Fuzzy rose onto tiptoe and gripped the cage bars, awaiting an answer.

"It's not—" Miss Wills began. A confused frown blanketed her face like a fog bank. "I don't know," she said at last. "I don't think so, but . . ."

The class erupted in side conversations. Fuzzy felt squirmy all over, like he'd gotten a case of mange mites.

Principal Flake was a nice lady, for a principal. She wouldn't *really* ban classroom pets.

Would she?

Clap-clap, clap-clap-clap! Miss Wills applauded in a rhythm, and the kids responded with an answering rhythm. Voices trailed away.

"I know we're all stirred up about this rumor," said the teacher. "But right now it's only that—a rumor. Rest assured that I will learn the truth and let you know."

"Soon?" asked Sofia.

"Soon as I can. And now, if you don't mind, maybe we can do some actual schoolwork?"

Students settled back into their seats. Fuzzy drew a long, shaky breath. As the class learned about the scientific method, he started applying it himself.

Evidence: People were saying Mrs. Flake might want to ban classroom pets.

Hypothesis: If that were true, something had turned the normally friendly woman against them.

Conclusion: Fuzzy and his friends had better turn her back into a pro-pet principal in a jiffy. Otherwise, they'd have to say good-bye to their students, their home, and their purpose in life.

Fuzzy eyed the wall clock. How could the minutes move so slowly when so much was on the line?

At long last, the students headed home, Miss Wills marched off to meet with the principal, and Fuzzy was left to wait for the custodian's daily visit. Up and down he paced, wearing a rut in the fresh pine shavings that lined his habitat.

When Mr. Darius arrived to tidy up, Fuzzy took heart in the fact that the lanky janitor didn't mention anything about a ban. He just fed Fuzzy some celery, swept the floor, and emptied trash cans, gliding on to the next room, as smooth as a dolphin's belly button.

The instant the door clicked shut, Fuzzy push-push-pushed his escape path together. Up went the platform against the cage wall. Snug beside it went wooden cubes and a ball.

In a rush, Fuzzy scrambled from blocks to ball to platform. Over the wall he wriggled, landing with a *whump* on the table. From there, he followed his usual path down to the floor, across to the cubbyholes, and up the plastic saguaro to the bookcase.

Just as he stepped onto the bookshelf, however, Fuzzy heard something that froze him in his tracks: a rattle in the keyhole!

Holy haystacks!

Pressing himself into a corner of the shelf, Fuzzy did his best impression of a hairy book.

Into the room strode Miss Wills, muttering to herself. Crossing to her desk, she fished her purse from a drawer and lifted her sweater off the back of her chair.

Fuzzy held his breath. Would she notice his escape?

His teacher marched toward the door. It was looking like she'd blow right past his cage. Fuzzy began to relax.

Then Miss Wills pivoted and leaned over his habitat.

Uh-oh.

She tapped on the bars. "Fuzzy? You in your igloo?"

Jaw clenched, Fuzzy hoped against hope that she didn't try to peek inside his favorite sleep spot. He *really* didn't want her to know he could escape.

"Don't worry, big guy," said the teacher. "It'll all work out somehow."

She patted the cage and headed straight out the door.

Fuzzy scrunched up his nose. What did she mean, *somehow*? With doubt wriggling in his belly like a mealworm casserole, Fuzzy scaled the rest of the bookcase, pushed aside a ceiling tile, and clambered up into the crawl space above.

He had to know whether the other pets had heard anything more about this possible threat. Fast as a furry thunderbolt, he galloped along through the drop ceiling, sneezing occasionally as he kicked up dust.

Before long, a warm amber light shone upward through the dimness. He found himself at the entrance to the class pets' clubhouse, a forgotten space above Room 2-B's closet. Voices echoed below. He wasn't the first to arrive.

Trotting down the narrow plank into the clubhouse, Fuzzy spotted most of the pets gathered around Cinnabun, their floppy-eared rabbit president.

"Simmer down, y'all," she was saying. "No need to get your whiskers in a tangle."

"Have you heard the rumor?" said Fuzzy, skidding down the ramp to join them.

"That they want you to star in an episode of *World's Weirdest Rodents?*" said Igor the green iguana. "Heard it."

Cinnabun tsk-tsked. "That's unkind, Brother Igor. If you mean the rumor about banning classroom pets, Brother Fuzzy, that's exactly what we were discussing."

"Is it true?" asked Fuzzy.

"I heard yes," said Sassafras the parakeet.

"I heard no," said Igor.

"I heard I might have to find myself a new crib," said Vinnie the rat, "and I don't like it."

Luther the rosy boa shrugged, sending a ripple down his powerful body. "In other word*sss*," he said, "nobody knows."

"Knows what?" squeaked a chipper voice. Mistletoe the mouse was scampering down the ramp, tail whipping behind her like a flag. "What'd I miss?"

"Nothin' much," said Vinnie. "Just that Principal Flake is maybe gonna boot us outta school."

Clutching her chest, Mistletoe staggered back a few steps. "Us?" she said. "Out?"

"That's the rumor, Little Bit," said Luther. He slithered up to a cat sculpture that had been salvaged from the trash and draped himself over it.

On shaky legs, the mouse tottered the rest of the way down to join the group. "B-but that's horror-ful!"

"There's been no announcement," said Cinnabun, patting Mistletoe's shoulder, "but somehow the word has spread all over school."

"A-are they allowed to *do* that?" asked Mistletoe.

"We don't know." Fuzzy tugged on his whiskers nervously. "But we've got to find out."

"Amen, brother," said the rabbit. "But how?"

For a few seconds, no one spoke. Then Luther drawled, "What we need is a *ssspy*—someone who can watch the principal and get the lowdown."

"But the secretary would never agree to spy for us," said Mistletoe. "She's too loyal."

Luther exchanged a glance with Fuzzy. "I was thinking of one of us," he said.

Fuzzy frowned. "But how can we get close enough to spy during school hours without being missed in our classrooms?"

"Beats me, Fuzzarino," said Luther. "I was kinda hoping *you'd* figure out that part."

"Thanks a lot," said Fuzzy.

Sassafras shook out her wings. "Meanwhile, we can't just wait around for our doom like pigeons on a ledge."

"That's right!" Igor pounded the box they used as a makeshift table. "We've got to strike back with all our might."

Cinnabun arched one perfect eyebrow. "Are you suggesting we assault Mrs. Flake?"

"If that's what it takes, then yeah!" cried Igor. "Storm the barricades!" For a cold-blooded creature, he got pretty hot under the collar sometimes.

"Sugar, you want to know the surest way to get kicked out of this school?"

"Not particularly," said Igor.

"Attack the principal," said Cinnabun. "Oh, no, I think we'll catch more flies with honey than with vinegar."

"Why are we catching flies?" came a creaky voice from above.

Fuzzy turned to see Marta the Russian tortoise creeping down the ramp.

"It's . . . a long story," he said.

"Principal Nutjob might ban all pets," said Vinnie. "We're tryin' to talk her out of it."

Fuzzy smirked. "Well, maybe not *that* long a story."

"Gather round, y'all, and let's put our heads together," said Cinnabun. "This is going to take all the brainpower we can muster."

CHAPTER 3

Picture Perfect

Like a dizzy bumblebee at a botanical garden, the debate meandered this way and that. Bribery, protests, and threats were all suggested and discarded. Someone even proposed holding a sit-in at the principal's office. But at last, Cinnabun came up with what she considered to be the perfect strategy.

"We'll charm her socks off," she said.

Mistletoe frowned. "I don't get it. Why her socks?"

"Figure of speech," said Fuzzy gently.

"She means we try beguiling Principal Flake into keeping us," said Marta.

"Oh," said the mouse. "That makes more sense."

Sassafras groomed her wing feathers. "But if we can't leave our cages during school, how do we get to the principal?"

That set off a fair bit of head scratching. Finally, Fuzzy snapped his fingers. "Photos," he said.

"Blackmail?" Igor asked doubtfully.

Vinnie gave a thumbs-up. "I like the way ya think."

"Not photos of her, photos of us," said Fuzzy.

"We blackmail ourselves?" said Mistletoe.

Fuzzy threw up his paws. "No, we take cute selfies and leave them in her mailbox. That way we can charm her without leaving our rooms."

"Bless your pea-pickin' heart," cried Cinnabun. "That's brilliant!"

"Well, I wouldn't go that far," said Vinnie. "But not bad, Parsley Breath. Not bad." He bopped Fuzzy on the shoulder.

"Only one problem," said Luther. "Unlesss one of you's been holding out, nobody has a picture-taking cell phone."

"No problem at all," said Cinnabun. "Miss Nakamura has an old-fashioned camera in her closet. It makes a photo right on the spot."

"Bingo-bongo!" crowed Sassafras. "What are we waiting for?"

Cinnabun, Sassafras, and Igor hustled off to fetch the camera, returning shortly with a funny-looking contraption like nothing Fuzzy had ever seen. It was wide, gray, and most un-camera-like.

"How's it work?" he asked dubiously.

"Here," said the bunny. "Hold this side of it, and I'll lift the other."

The camera was surprisingly heavy. Still, Fuzzy and Cinnabun managed to heft the device and aim it. The rabbit squinted through a tiny window at Mistletoe. "All right, sweet girl. Smile and say 'shoofly pie!'"

The mouse obliged, and Cinnabun pressed a button on the back.

Click! Whirrrr went the camera. Fuzzy nearly dropped it when a stiff little sheet of paper stuck out the front like a square tongue.

Taking the image in his paws, Vinnie squinted at it. "Ya sure this antique still works?" he said. "Yer picture's a dud. All we got is fog."

Setting down the camera, Fuzzy came to peer over his shoulder. Slower than a sloth in summertime, a dim shape was emerging on the gray paper.

"A ghost!" Mistletoe pointed with a shaking finger.

"*Your* ghost," said Igor, craning his neck to see.

And bit by bit, the mouse's face took form. After a minute more, they were all staring at an image of a grinning Mistletoe.

"Coolio!" squeaked the mouse.

"Not bad," said Igor, "except for that smile. Ugh." He made an exaggerated shudder, and Fuzzy poked him with an elbow.

Brushing her paws together, Cinnabun said, "One down, seven to go. And I'm next!"

One by one, all the pets had their photos taken, and one by one, their images emerged. Rather than striking an adorable pose, Luther opted for "harmless," because, as he said, "Snakes don't do cute."

Using crayons borrowed from a kindergarten classroom, each pet wrote a message on the white border at the bottom of his or her photo, like:

Pets are cool,
Pets love you, and
Criminals hate snakes (Luther's contribution).

When everyone had finished, Fuzzy, Luther, and Vinnie volunteered to carry the photos to the office and leave them in the principal's mail cubbyhole. Off they headed through the crawl space, toting their precious cargo.

As the three of them neared the office, Vinnie asked, "So whattaya think? Does this harebrained scheme stand a snowball's chance?"

"Gee, thanks for the vote of confidence," said Fuzzy.

Luther smirked. "Harebrained it might be, but we've got to start somewhere."

"Look, some dames like the mushy stuff, and some don't," said the rat. "All I'm askin', is Flake the type that would fall for it?"

Fuzzy cocked his head. "Hard to say. But she did protect you when that assistant janitor wanted to chop you up like broccoli."

"That's true."

"So she's either got a *sss*oft heart or a *sss*oft head." Luther grinned.

"Oh, har-de-har," said Vinnie.

Prying up a ceiling tile, Fuzzy poked his nose through to see if they'd reached the office yet—and froze, stock-still. Adrenaline pumped through his veins like a spring-time flood.

Directly below, he recognized a familiar, close-cropped head: Mr. Darius. The janitor was wiping down the table, whistling a tune.

"What's the holdup?" asked Vinnie.

"Shhh!" Fuzzy hissed, as loudly as he dared.

"Ya paintin' a picture or what?" said the rat, even louder.

Fuzzy shushed him again, frantically waving one paw for quiet.

Below, Mr. Darius straightened. His head swiveled this way and that.

Don't look up, don't look up, thought Fuzzy.

And then, in a motion that made Fuzzy's stomach drop, the janitor craned his neck and began to look up.

Too late to replace the ceiling tile. *Zip!* Fuzzy ducked back out of sight.

Had the janitor spotted him? Mr. Darius had turned a blind eye the last time he'd caught Fuzzy out of his cage, but this time he might not be so forgiving.

"Huh," said the janitor. "What happened here?"

Putting a finger to his lips, Fuzzy glared at Luther and Vinnie. Both pets held still.

The scrape and creak of a chair being moved into place drifted up from below. Fuzzy nearly jumped out of his skin when Mr. Darius's hand grabbed the ceiling tile beside him.

Would the man investigate further?

Fuzzy held his breath. The moment stretched like a spandex skirt on an elephant seal. Then the light from below winked out as the janitor slid the tile back into place.

Fuzzy sagged in relief. Vinnie mimed wiping sweat off his forehead. Luther looked as cool as ever.

The three pets put an ear to the ceiling tiles and listened for the telltale door closing that meant Mr. Darius had moved on to another room. At last it came. They gave him another minute to leave the area, then lifted the tile again.

Poking his head through the gap, Luther checked things out. "Clear as a cube of sunshine," came his muffled voice.

Fuzzy and Vinnie carefully dropped the photos onto the workroom table below. Then, all three pets jumped onto a high bookcase and clambered down it to the tabletop.

Once they reclaimed the photos, Fuzzy and his friends had a few rough moments figuring out how to get their pictures up to the mail cubbyhole. But escape artist Luther came through in the crunch. By wrapping his tail around the staff refrigerator's handle, he was able to dangle downward and accept the photos in his mouth, then twine upward and deposit them into Mrs. Flake's box.

Vinnie clapped. "Impressive moves, Mr. Forky Tongue. Do ya also like to limbo?"

"Not for love or money," said Luther.

Quickly and quietly, the three pets retraced their path back to the bookcase and up to the ceiling. As he slid the tile into place after them, Fuzzy had a moment of doubt. Would the charm approach really change the principal's mind?

It had better, he decided. The alternative was too awful to contemplate.

CHAPTER 4

From Bad to Nurse

Over the next two days, the pets went all out with their charm offensive. They laboriously scrawled anonymous pro-pet letters and delivered them to the principal's mailbox. They tried to look extra-winsome whenever Mrs. Flake happened to visit one of their classrooms.

They even attempted to sweeten her up by leaving cafeteria cookies on her desk. (Mistletoe reported that ants got to these before Mrs. Flake did.)

But after two days, no results. Rumors still swirled, and by Thursday, the pets still had no evidence that their efforts were softening Principal Flake's heart. Fuzzy was so keyed up, he spent that morning pacing around his habitat.

When Miss Wills noticed this, she went over to his cage, crouching so they were eye to eye. "Is something bothering you, big guy?"

Fuzzy had to restrain himself from rolling his eyes. *Was something bothering him?* Oh, not much. Only the death of happiness, the loss of purpose, and the possible end of his career as a classroom pet.

"Is he sick?" asked Heavy-Handed Jake, who sat nearest to Fuzzy's cage.

The teacher frowned. "I'm not sure. Sometimes when guinea pigs pace like that, it's a sign that something's wrong."

Something's wrong, all right, thought Fuzzy. *But it's not a simple case of scurvy.*

"Will Fuzzy be going to the vet?" asked Sofia.

"If he keeps it up," said Miss Wills. "But first I'd take him to see Mr. Wong."

Zoey-with-the-braces crinkled her nose. "Our school nurse? Um, doesn't he only help *people*?"

"Not always." Miss Wills straightened, brushing back her bangs. "Before he worked in schools, Mr. Wong used to be a vet's assistant. Let's keep an eye on Fuzzy. If his symptoms continue, Mr. Wong can check him out."

Fuzzy turned away. Their hearts were in the right place, but it wouldn't do him a lick of good to see the school nurse, whose room was in the main office, right across from the principal's . . .

Fuzzy's jaw dropped. Luther's idea of setting a spy in the office flashed through his mind, and he put a paw to his chest.

Leaning across his desk, Jake stared at Fuzzy. "Is that one of his symptoms?"

"No," said Miss Wills. "Probably just gas."

"So what do we look for?" asked Sofia.

The teacher glanced from Fuzzy to her students. "Watch for behaviors like circling the cage, hiding, chewing on the bars, and over-grooming."

Suddenly, Fuzzy wanted nothing more than to visit Mr. Wong. He decided to give the kids all the symptoms they could handle.

After Miss Wills returned to the front of the room and resumed her lesson, Fuzzy went back to circling his cage. He paced around, and around, and around, and around . . . until he was good and dizzy.

Heavy-Handed Jake nudged Sofia and pointed at Fuzzy. So far, so good.

Next, Fuzzy began gnawing on the bars of his habitat. *Yuck*. Honestly, how could other guinea pigs stand this? The metal tasted bitter and harsh—nothing at all like yummy parsley.

Zoey-with-the braces watched him closely.

Finally, Fuzzy took a break from bar biting and groomed himself for a while. *Lickety-lickety-lickety-slurp*. Even his own fur tasted better than the metal, although he accidentally swallowed some of it and had to hack it back up with a *hyakk-hyock-hyeww*. Fuzzy pasted a woeful expression on his face.

That did it. Three hands shot into the air.

"Miss Wills! Miss Wills!"

The teacher called on Zoey.

"Fuzzy's been doing all those things you mentioned," said the girl. "Plus, he's even coughing!"

"Oh my." Miss Wills glanced at Fuzzy. He favored her with an extra-pitiful look and coughed again for good measure.

"I'll take him up to see Mr. Wong," said the teacher, hurrying over to Fuzzy's habitat. "Class, turn to page 180 in *Reflections on America* and read about the lead-up to the Civil War. I won't be long."

And with that, Miss Wills reached down and collected Fuzzy in a secure two-handed grip. She definitely had the softest hands of anyone who'd ever carried him.

Together, they left the room and hurried down the halls toward the office. As they went, Miss Wills muttered, "I can't believe you're sick. I try to feed you right, give you lots of love and exercise . . ."

Fuzzy winced. It bugged him that Miss Wills thought she'd failed him. Far from it. She was the best human a guinea pig could hope for. But desperate times called for desperate measures.

He rubbed his head against her hand, trying to offer some comfort.

"Aw, don't worry, big guy," she said. "We'll have you feeling back in the pink in no time."

Fuzzy didn't know what pinkness had to do with anything, but he appreciated her concern.

When they entered the office, the school secretary, Mrs. Gomez, was sitting at the counter. She glanced up from a stack of forms.

"What's with your little friend?" she asked.

"We're not sure," said Miss Wills. "Is Mr. Wong in?"

The secretary gestured with her pen. "Go right ahead."

As they headed down the hall, Fuzzy peered about with interest. The office smelled of magic markers, muffins, and burnt coffee. Its cheery, butter-yellow walls were plastered with safety posters, flyers for school events, and a row of old-timey portraits. Fuzzy figured these were of people who'd been around when the school was built, way back before the dawn of time.

Then he spotted his own face. What the . . . ? Fuzzy only had time to read the poster's SAVE OUR PETS headline before he was whisked down the hall. His spirits lifted like that floaty thing in a toilet tank. Somebody was on their side!

Miss Wills passed the teachers' workroom, which Fuzzy recognized from his after-school field trip with

Vinnie and Luther. Just past that, she zeroed in on a half-open door on the left, but Fuzzy was more interested in the door on the right.

That door boasted a big frosted glass panel in its top half. Stenciled on the glass in golden letters was PRINCIPAL KIMBERLY FLAKE, and behind it, Fuzzy could see the dim shape of the principal herself, talking on the telephone at her desk.

He strained to overhear her conversation. Nothing but mumbles.

Miss Wills rapped on the nurse's door. "Knock, knock? Paul, you there?"

"Come on in," said a man's voice. "We're just finishing up."

As they entered the room, Fuzzy grimaced at the sharp tang of disinfectant. A curly-haired boy sat on the exam table with his elbow held forward and a world-class pout on his face. Tears streaked his cheeks.

"Ouchie-ouch!" he cried as a lean man with thick, short-cropped hair put a Band-Aid on his arm.

"There, all better," the school nurse said.

"Hurts." The boy snuffled.

Mr. Wong ruffled his hair. "Aw, come on, kiddo. I thought you were Iron Man. Does Iron Man cry at every little boo-boo?"

"Um, no?" said the boy, wiping his runny nose on the sleeve of what Fuzzy now saw was a superhero T-shirt.

"That's right, Devon. He just brushes himself off and gets right back into it."

A tentative grin spread on Devon's face. "Yeah, he does." The boy slid off the table and headed for the door.

"Just be careful out there," the nurse called after him.

With a quick backward wave, the boy was gone. Off to stir up more trouble, Fuzzy had no doubt.

"So, Jessica," said Mr. Wong, "what's up? Here to practice your dance moves?" He did a little shoulder shimmy.

Miss Wills laughed. "I'll save those for Zumba class. No, Fuzzy has been acting funny today."

Leaning forward, Mr. Wong extended a finger to scratch behind Fuzzy's ears. "This little guy? He was born funny."

Fuzzy knew he was being teased, but somehow he didn't mind. The scratching helped.

"He's been pacing around his cage, chewing on the bars, and coughing," said Miss Wills. "I'm worried. Could you take a quick look at him?"

Mr. Wong touched the teacher's arm. "For you, anything."

"Thanks." Handing Fuzzy over to the nurse, Miss Wills said, "I have to get back to class. Can you keep him here for a bit? I'll claim him at lunchtime."

"Can do," said Mr. Wong. "Your little fuzzball will be safe with me."

The paper cover crinkled as the nurse set him down on the pallet. When he turned to fetch his instruments, Fuzzy took the opportunity to look around. The room was decorated in greens and pale blues. Posters proclaiming THE FLU AND YOU, YOUR HEALTHY DIET, and THE DEPARTMENT OF OWIES! covered the walls. The place smelled of fear, disinfectant, and cherry lollipops.

Despite himself, Fuzzy gave a little shudder.

"Now, let's see what's up with you," said Mr. Wong. Placing two earbud-looking thingies in his ears, he lifted the metal disk attached to the other end of a length of rubber. The nurse cradled Fuzzy expertly. "This may be a teensy bit chilly," he said, placing the disk on his chest.

Wheek! Fuzzy squealed, wriggling like mad. *Chilly?* That thing was colder than skinny-dipping in Antarctica.

The nurse listened intently for a few heartbeats. When he slid the icy metal down to listen to the lungs, Fuzzy wiggled again. Mr. Wong poked and prodded him in various places.

"Eee-hee-hee, that tickles!" cried Fuzzy.

"Hold still, buddy," said the nurse. He peered into Fuzzy's ears, eyes, and mouth. "Good so far," he muttered, setting him down again. "Now, let's see if I still have one of those special thermometers . . ."

When he heard that, Fuzzy involuntarily clenched his lower cheeks. He remembered all too well how vets take a pet's temperature.

Just then, Mrs. Gomez poked her head through the doorway. "One of the kindergarteners had an accident on the playground. Could you . . . ?"

"On my way." Abandoning his quest for a thermometer, the nurse glanced around the room. He cleared out some boxes of bandages from the top tub of a three-tiered storage rack and tossed them aside. "Okay, mister." Lifting Fuzzy off the exam table, Mr. Wong set him in the tub. "You stay put while I'm gone."

The nurse hustled out the door, pulling it shut behind him. But it didn't quite close.

Shweek-shweek-shweek squeaked Mr. Wong's sneakers as he hustled down the hall. The door hung open about two inches—more than enough for some daring rodent to squeeze through and investigate.

Fuzzy grinned.

It just so happened that Daring Rodent was his middle name.

CHAPTER 5

Spy Hard

Rearing up onto his hind legs, Fuzzy peered over the edge of the little tub the nurse had left him in. *Hmm.* Too far to jump. He cast around for an exit path and noticed the metal frame that supported the three storage containers.

Perfect.

Clambering over the edge, Fuzzy wrapped his arms and legs around the rod, sliding down like it was a firefighter's pole.

Schoomp! He landed safely on the nubbly carpet. Scurrying over to the door, Fuzzy put an eye to the crack.

"—Appreciate your seeing me again." A nasal voice as sharp as two-year-old cheddar cheese filled the short hallway.

"Not at all," came Principal Flake's voice.

A second later, two pairs of legs flashed into view just outside the door. Fuzzy ducked back out of sight.

"This issue is not going away," said Sharp Voice, "and I'd like to know your plans for dealing with it."

"Let's discuss this in my office, Mrs. Krumpton," said the principal.

Fuzzy risked another quick peek. A tall, blonde woman in a fancy leather jacket and burgundy slacks was being ushered into the room across the hall. She towered over the shorter, thicker, older Mrs. Flake.

Time to spy. Maybe the two women would drop some kind of clue about the class pets' fate.

They stepped into Mrs. Flake's office, and the door shut behind them. Suddenly, their voices were muffled, like moles having an underground chitchat.

Wiggling whiskers! Fuzzy would have to get much closer if he wanted to hear.

Ever so slowly, he nosed into the gap, nudging open

the nurse's door. When his head was sticking out, he quickly scanned right and left—and froze.

Tok-tok-tok. Down the hall strode Mrs. Gomez, her thick heels rapping out a rhythm. Fuzzy waited until she'd rounded the corner and resumed her seat before even twitching a whisker.

After one last check, he pushed the rest of the way through the door. The hallway was deserted. Across the corridor he scooted.

Fuzzy pushed on Mrs. Flake's door. No luck. It was shut tight. Placing his ear up against the wood, he caught muffled conversation.

"—Can't believe you haven't taken action yet," came Mrs. Krumpton's piercing voice. "This is a serious threat."

"A threat?" The principal sounded skeptical. "That sounds rather—"

"These animals have no place in school. No value. They're distracting and dangerous and full of disease."

Fuzzy growled low in his throat. Lies! All lies! Pets were loyal and helpful and—well, okay, maybe he did have that case of mange mites once, but it went away.

"I appreciate your concerns," said Principal Flake. "And I've discussed them with the teachers who have pets in their classrooms."

"Talk is cheap," said Mrs. Krumpton. "The PTA wants action!"

A chair creaked. "Look, please try to understand," said Mrs. Flake in a reasonable tone. "Classroom pets are a longstanding tradition here at Leo Gumpus. They've even been approved by the school board."

"The board can change its policies."

"True," said Mrs. Flake, "but you don't overturn a school's traditions without getting input from all affected parties."

"Talk and more talk." Mrs. Krumpton's voice had more sharp edges than a sculpture made of scissors. "Sounds like you're not confident of your authority. Are you the principal or not?"

A throat cleared. "Really, Mrs. Krumpton. There's no need to be rude."

"I'm not rude—I'm direct," said the PTA woman. "One of your precious pets caused an accident, and my friend's son was injured."

Fuzzy's cheeks went warm with the sudden realization. She was talking about *him*.

"From what I've heard," the principal said, "it was only a bump on the head. This sort of thing happens every day on the playground. You can hardly blame the pet."

Fuzzy bit his lip. No need to blame the pet; the pet was blaming himself.

"I find your whole approach very disappointing," snapped Mrs. Krumpton. "I don't believe you're giving this the weight it deserves."

"I can assure you I am," said the principal.

"Actions speak louder than words. If you don't do something about this by next week, I've decided to call an all-school meeting to change the pets policy."

Fuzzy's hackles rose. This was serious stuff. How could one little incident lead to so much trouble?

"You can't do that," said Principal Flake.

"Oh, no?" said Mrs. Krumpton. "I am the PTA president."

Mrs. Flake's voice grew steely. "And the PTA serves under the principal's authority."

A chair scraped in the office. "You don't want to get into a tussle with me over some silly animals," said the PTA woman. "I've got friends in high places. It could end quite badly."

"For whom?" said Principal Flake in a voice colder than a January moon.

The women sounded closer—too close.

Fuzzy jumped, jolted out of his guilty reverie.

Footsteps scuffed. The door could open any second. Galvanized with fright, he darted across the corridor just as the office doorknob turned.

"I look forward to hearing of your plans to protect our children," Mrs. Krumpton was saying as she stepped into the hallway.

Fuzzy only just managed to slip into the nurse's room in time. He sagged against the doorframe.

"Caring for students is our top priority. Thanks for coming in," said the principal in a tone that managed to sound like *Go stick your head in a bucket of goo* even if the words themselves were technically polite.

When Fuzzy peeked through the crack, he saw the PTA president stalking away, her back stiffer than a concrete cardigan. Mrs. Flake stared after the woman, her expression troubled.

Returning to the storage rack, Fuzzy tried to scale the metal rod back up into the tub. He discovered why firefighters take the pole down but the stairs up. On his third time sliding back to the floor, he heard a footfall behind him.

"Ah, we have an escape artist," said Mr. Wong. "Naughty guinea pig!"

Busted. Fuzzy sighed.

A pair of warm hands closed around him, lifting him into the air. "Emily, honey, go sit on that chair for a second," said the nurse to a tearstained kindergartener. "Mr. Fuzzy and I have one last piece of unfinished business."

Fuzzy wondered what that could be. The nurse had given him a pretty thorough examination already.

Cradling him on his back like a baby, Mr. Wong reached for a small thermometer with a handle. "Just relax," he said. "This won't hurt a bit."

Fuzzy gritted his teeth and clenched his cheeks, recognizing a little white lie when he heard one.

CHAPTER 6

The Hunger Games

Waiting through the rest of that long day was like trying to stay cool on a bed of coals. It was seven shades of awful. How could things have gotten this bad, this quickly? That mean PTA president really had it in for them, and she seemed to be forcing a showdown with the principal—all because Fuzzy had tried to help Malik.

His stomach churned and his throat felt tight. If Fuzzy could have undone his actions, he would have. But since he couldn't, at least he could figure out how to deal with the situation.

Or not. Three hours of thinking produced only a throbbing headache.

Maybe Cinnabun or one of the others would know what to do. Fuzzy sure didn't. After school, he accepted his usual treat from Mr. Darius with good grace, but all his attention was focused on solving the problem.

"What's wrong, little buddy?" said the janitor, stroking his back. "You seem a million miles away."

"I'm in a heap of trouble," Fuzzy moaned, even though he knew the man couldn't understand.

Mr. Darius shook his head. "Sometimes I really wish I could speak guinea pig."

"Me too," said Fuzzy. "Every single day."

When the janitor had moved on to the next classroom, Fuzzy performed his usual escape routine. He trotted through the crawl space toward the pets' clubhouse, burdened with his bad news.

When he told the others what he'd overheard in the office, the reactions were as predictable as a sunrise.

"She *what*?" yelped Igor.

"After all my years as a class pet, they want to throw me out into the cold?" said Marta the tortoise.

"No way, no how!" cried Igor.

"Humans." Vinnie made a face like biting into a rotten mango. "Ya just can't trust 'em."

"That witch deserves a lash of my tail!" growled Igor.

Cinnabun raised her paws in a calming gesture. "I don't think whipping the PTA president will change her mind."

"Maybe not," said Igor, "but it'd cheer *me* up."

"What in the wide world of sports does this woman have against us?" squawked Sassafras. Fuzzy shrugged guiltily. He just couldn't bring himself to tell her that his actions had inspired Mrs. Krumpton's anti-pet campaign.

Through it all, Mistletoe remained silent, eyes huge, both paws clapped over her mouth.

"Are you okay?" Fuzzy asked.

The mouse shook her head. "If they kick me out of school, Mr. Broxton will take me back to the pet store."

"So?" said Vinnie. "There're worse fates."

Mistletoe's eyes welled with unshed tears. "Not for me. Mice are a dime a dozen. The pet store will probably sell me off to get fed to a—a snake." She glanced at the boa. "No offense, Luther."

"None taken," he said. "You *are* pretty yummy looking."

The mouse blanched.

"Kidding, kidding," Luther said. "Thi*sss* boa never eats friends."

Fuzzy wrung his paws. "Can we stop talking about who's eating who, and start figuring out how to keep us all from ending up back at the pet store?"

"Thinking caps on!" squawked Sassafras.

Cinnabun pouted prettily. "But what about our charm campaign?"

"It's just not enough," said Fuzzy. "Principal Flake is on the fence. How else can we convince her?"

For a minute or two, the clubhouse was silent as the pets paced, scratched themselves, or stared into space, thinking.

Then Marta raised her head. "A hunger strike," she said.

"Say what?" Luther asked.

"Mrs. Twain likes to watch documentaries," said the tortoise. "We saw this one about a human named Gandhi, how he would fast to protest unfairness."

Igor's eyes goggled. "Let me get this straight," he said. "This dude *deliberately* didn't eat anything?"

"It's called nonviolent resistance," said Marta.

The iguana snorted. "It'd never work. Being hungry would *make* me violent."

But Cinnabun had that light in her eyes that signaled she was considering the idea. "I like the nonviolent way."

Vinnie scoffed. "I don't usually agree with Turkey Neck over there,"—he hooked a thumb at Igor—"but I gotta say he's right. This bunch? Goin' without food?"

"Why ever not?" said the rabbit.

Half the room had plenty of reasons why not. She let the pets rant for a while, then rapped her gavel on the president's podium (actually a thick copy of *The Complete Works of William Shakespeare*).

"Are y'all saying you wouldn't pass up a few meals to save our way of life?" she asked.

Sassafras hung her head. "Well . . ."

"That's exactly what I'm sayin'," said Vinnie. "It ain't natural."

Cinnabun nodded. "And that's precisely the point. That's why it would get their attention."

"I don't know . . ." Igor screwed up his face.

Fuzzy felt like he needed to weigh in. Maybe this wasn't the best idea in the world, but it was an idea. "I think it could work," he said. "Why don't we try it?"

"Just for Friday and the weekend," said Mistletoe quickly. "What's the harm?"

Twirling her gavel, Cinnabun said, "Brother Fuzzy has made a motion that we hold a hunger strike to achieve our goals. All in favor?"

Slowly, reluctantly, most of the pets raised a paw, a wing, or a tail. Only Vinnie and Igor abstained.

Bomp, bomp! The gavel pounded. "Majority rules," said Cinnabun. "Motion carried."

Sassafras made a face. "When do we start?"

"Tomorrow morning," said the rabbit president.

"Then I know what I'm doing tonight," said Vinnie.

"A pig-out to end all pig-outs," said Igor. "Let's munch!"

The next morning, it took every ounce of willpower Fuzzy had to turn up his nose at his food dish full of sweet timothy hay. Every fiber of his being urged him to stick his face in the bowl and gobble, gobble, gobble. Instead, he just walked away.

"Hey, Miss Wills," said Kaylee, who was on feeding duty that week. "Fuzzy doesn't want to eat."

With a frown, the teacher paused her science lesson. "Really?"

"Yeah, he won't touch his food," said Kaylee. "And the hay is super fresh, too."

"That's odd," said Miss Wills. "He's never done that before."

"So maybe he's sick," said Amir.

Miss Wills shook her head. "Mr. Wong said Fuzzy was just fine, everything normal. Unless . . ."

"What?" said Abby.

"Unless something's seriously wrong, and he couldn't detect it."

Someone gasped. Fuzzy rolled his eyes. The only thing wrong with him was that his stomach was growling like a cave full of bears after a long winter. This hunger strike wasn't quite going according to plan.

"Should we take him to the vet?" asked Spiky Diego.

Miss Wills walked over to the cage and regarded Fuzzy gravely. He tried his best to look healthy and bright-eyed.

"Let's give him until the end of the day," she said. "Maybe he's just having an off morning." Returning to the front of the room, Miss Wills resumed her lessons.

As the hours crept onward, Fuzzy's hunger pangs grew worse. It felt like a tapeworm was twanging away on the strings of his gut. And no matter where he went in his habitat, no matter how he tried to distract himself, the sweet smell of the timothy hay followed him everywhere.

Eeeeat meeee, it called. *IIII'm taaasteee!*

Fuzzy gritted his teeth against temptation. He chewed on his wooden block, but all that did was get his belly juices flowing. He told himself, *Don't think of hay,* but of course that guaranteed that hay was all he could think about.

Finally, Miss Wills and the students went to go eat lunch—*lunch!*—and Fuzzy was left alone with his thoughts and his gurgling gut. Taking up a position in the cage as far from the hay as possible, he tried to think calming thoughts.

But hunger had left him lightheaded. He began to hallucinate. Fuzzy thought he saw Geronimo the rat, former president of the class pets, waving to him from the teacher's desk.

"No need to punish yourself," said Geronimo.

"I thought you'd retired to a farm," said Fuzzy.

"Nobody's around," said the rat. "You're all alone. Who would know if you took just a teensy taste of that hay?"

Fuzzy's empty belly weighed in, saying, *Listen to the rat.*

"But we're on a hunger strike," he protested. "We all promised not to eat anything."

The rat hallucination chuckled. "Do you think those other pets are going hungry? I bet Igor didn't last two minutes."

This was true. Igor would eat anything. One time, Fuzzy even saw him snacking on an eraser, which Fuzzy was pretty sure had no nutritional value.

"No, I shouldn't . . ." said Fuzzy. "I promised."

Geronimo grinned his crooked grin. "What would one bite hurt?" And then he faded away, leaving only a faint impression of whiskers in the air.

A sudden hunger pang, sharp as a fresh X-ACTO blade, wracked Fuzzy's poor tummy. A thought struck him. *What if humans could fast but guinea pigs couldn't?* Maybe it was actually *dangerous* for him to go without food for too long.

How would I know? he thought. *I'm only a rodent.*

Fuzzy looked over at the hay. So fresh, so tempting. He glanced back to where Geronimo's apparition had been. Could the rat be right?

What would it hurt to have just one sprig of hay? After all, he could go right back to fasting afterward, and nobody would ever know . . .

Whistling under his breath, Fuzzy ambled in the direction of his food bowl. As he passed by, he leaned over and took just the tiniest nibble of hay.

Wiggling whiskers!

It was good. It was *amazingly* good.

More! roared his stomach.

Fuzzy glanced around. The room was still empty. The sweet taste filled his mouth, making his taste buds dance the boogaloo. Surely one more bite wouldn't be such a big deal. He nibbled another mouthful of hay.

And another.

And *another*.

Fuzzy's head spun. The world narrowed to just the sight and taste and crunch of hay.

Mm-*mmm*.

A minute or so later, Fuzzy came back to himself. He was lying on his back beside the upended food bowl. Rolling over, he checked inside it. Empty.

Fuzzy sat up. Someone had eaten all his food.

Realization dawned.

He had eaten all his food.

Groaning, Fuzzy sank his head into his paws. His belly was happy, but his conscience was hurting.

How could he have broken the hunger strike after only half a day? And with all that was at stake? *Bad* guinea pig. Fuzzy was sure the other pets had been much more disciplined.

He sighed. He had a whole weekend to forget about his failure, but somehow Fuzzy knew he would never hear the end of it at Monday's Class Pets Club meeting.

CHAPTER 7

Old Stinky Whiskers's Bright Idea

"That was a terrible idea!" roared Igor as soon as the pets had assembled in their clubhouse Monday afternoon.

Cinnabun frowned. Even her frowns were adorable. "Did you try fasting?"

"Of course I tried," said the iguana. "I wrestled with myself for three whole minutes."

"That long?" said Sassafras drily. "Poor baby."

Igor gripped the sides of his spiky head. "It was torture. I'm still recovering."

Nodding sagely, Vinnie said, "What'd I tell ya? It's against animal nature."

"How long did you last?" Fuzzy asked the rat.

Vinnie shrugged. "I didn't even try. Pointless."

Fuzzy felt a little better about his own failings.

"Did anyone fast all weekend?" asked Cinnabun. No response. "How about all day Friday?"

Fuzzy surveyed the group. Only Luther raised his tail.

"I eat once a week, baby," he said.

Their rabbit president shook her head ruefully. "So much for our hunger strike."

The pets slumped, studying the floor, the pillows— anything but Cinnabun's disappointed gaze. Fuzzy found himself secretly glad that he wasn't the only one with no willpower.

"You know," said Marta gently, "I'm not sure it would've worked anyway."

"Why not?" asked Cinnabun.

"When I fasted all morning, they didn't think I was on a hunger strike," said the tortoise. "They thought I was sick."

"Me too," said Fuzzy.

Cinnabun blew out a sigh. "I guess we overlooked one teeny-weeny problem with the hunger strike approach."

"What's that?" said Mistletoe.

"Since we can't speak human, they had no idea we were fasting."

All the pets agreed that this was true. It was so easy to see—in hindsight, anyway. They sprawled around their clubhouse in attitudes of defeat.

Fuzzy gnawed on a whisker. Their campaign wasn't going so well. At this rate, mean Mrs. Krumpton would call that all-school meeting, and their time at Leo Gumpus would be over faster than a cheetah's coffee break.

Guilt weighed Fuzzy down like a stone in his stomach. One lousy misstep on his part had brought them to this place.

After all they'd been through, could this really be the end of the class pets?

Fuzzy stiffened his spine and gritted his teeth. The end? Not if he could help it. If Fuzzy had gotten his friends into this spot, he could darned well get them *out*.

Closing his eyes, he pictured the principal and the PTA president, and considered all he'd overheard at the office. Then something occurred to him.

"Listen," said Fuzzy. "Maybe we're going at this the wrong way."

"What do you mean?" asked Mistletoe. "Should we be violent?"

The iguana scowled. "After all that crazy fasting, I'm ready to take it out on somebody."

Fuzzy held up a palm. "No, I don't mean *how* we're doing this, I mean *who* we're doing it to."

Sassafras groomed her wing. "I don't follow."

Climbing to his feet, Fuzzy padded around the clubhouse. He always thought more clearly when he was moving. Or chewing.

"Maybe the principal's not the one we should be winning over," he said.

"But she's the most powerful person at school," said Sassafras. "Everyone knows that."

Fuzzy cocked his head. "Is she really?"

Uncoiling himself, Luther lifted his brow. "What are you getting at, Fuzzmeister?"

"From what I overheard, the PTA has lots of power too," said Fuzzy.

"True," said Cinnabun. She nibbled a fruit chew thoughtfully. "But the PTA is a whole passel of humans. By the time we convince all of them, it'll be too late."

Fuzzy scowled. He hadn't thought of that. But it seemed like he was on the right track, somehow. What was he missing?

Scratching himself with a hind paw, Vinnie squinted. "Who says we gotta win over the whole freakin' PTA?"

"Go on," said Cinnabun.

"Seems to me that this Krumpton dame is the key," said the rat. "If we can change her mind, she stops leaning on Principal Flake. Bim-bam-boom—problem solved."

He broke off a chunk of PowerBar, tossed it into the air, and caught it in his mouth.

The other pets looked at one another, then back at Vinnie.

"Never thought I'd say this," said Igor, "but ol' Stinky Whiskers just might be onto something."

Fuzzy's eyes lit up. "Of course," he said. "After all, Mrs. Krumpton only got involved because I made Malik—uh, because Malik's mom is a friend of hers, and she's against pets."

Marta gave him a thoughtful look but didn't speak.

Fuzzy hurried on, hoping that the rest of the pets hadn't noticed his slip. "The other PTA members might not even know about her plan yet. Mrs. Krumpton is the key."

Slithering over to a pillow and draping himself across it, Luther asked, "*Ssso* what would change Missy PTA's mind?"

Fuzzy bit his lip, reflecting on the woman's strong opinions. "A tank?"

Vinnie scoffed. "C'mon, Parsley Breath. Everyone's got a weak spot. We just gotta figure out what hers is."

"And how do we do that?" asked Mistletoe, who'd mostly been keeping quiet.

Gnawing on another chunk of PowerBar, Vinnie examined its wrapper. "Ya know, I'm almost getting used to these."

"Focus, Brother Vinnie," suggested Cinnabun.

"Right, right," said the rat. He stared up at the ceiling. "Hmm. Maybe there's somethin' in her past we could blackmail her with?"

"Now you're talking," said Igor.

"No time for that kind of research," said Fuzzy. "We need to stop her before the all-school meeting, and that could come any day now."

"If only we knew somethin' about this dame," said Vinnie. "Then we'd have an easier time figuring out our approach."

"Her child," said Marta. The old tortoise hadn't spoken in so long, Mistletoe jumped at the sound of her voice.

Side conversations faltered. Everyone turned to look at Marta.

"What about her kid?" asked Sassafras, shaking out her tail feathers.

"Humans adore their children," said the tortoise. "They save, they sacrifice, they even serve on the PTA for them. Maybe her child is her weakness."

Vinnie shook his head admiringly. "And here I thought that whole thing about old turtles being wise was just a cliché."

"I'm a tortoise," said Marta.

"Whatever," said the rat. "Either way, you've got smarts, lady."

Marta ducked her head, acknowledging the compliment.

Fuzzy brightened. "Now all we have to do is figure out who her kid is."

"Leave that to me," said Sassafras. "I know just where they keep those student files in the office." Her face darkened. "Although I might have some trouble getting into the cabinet."

Vinnie cracked his knuckles. "That's my department," he said. "Not a lock in the world can keep out this rat."

"That's settled, then," said Cinnabun. "Sister Sassafras and Brother Vinnie will go investigate and report back to us. Since this is a matter of some urgency, I suggest we wait right here for their return."

Prompted by his guilty conscience, Fuzzy stepped forward. "Um, I'll go with them." Watching him, Marta pursed her lips.

"You don't need to come," said Sassafras.

"Oh, but I want to," said Fuzzy. His conscience gave another twinge. "More hands, more eyes, more better."

Cinnabun's dimples sprouted. "I question your grammar, Brother Fuzzy, but I love your team spirit."

He flashed her a weak smile. "Then what are we waiting for? Let's start snooping."

CHAPTER 8

Filing for Dollars

Fuzzy had been visiting the office so much lately, he felt like they should give him his own desk and ID badge: *Mr. Fuzzy, School Sneak.* He led the way through the crawl space. Like spies on a mission, the three pets slipped along—silent, serious, and determined. Fuzzy didn't know what the others were thinking, but that nagging inner voice kept reminding him that this whole mess was his fault, and that he'd better find a solution soon.

He tried to ignore it. Fuzzy felt pressured enough already.

Onward they traipsed through the dusty drop ceiling, until Vinnie raised a paw. "We're here," he whispered. "I'm gonna take a peek, see if the coast is clear."

Sassafras made the okay sign with her wingtip feathers. Fuzzy was impressed at her dexterity.

Easing one of the ceiling tiles aside, Vinnie peered through the crack. He must not have seen anyone, because he stuck his whole head through the gap.

"The joint's deserted," he said, pulling himself back up. "If we go about two tiles thataway, we'll have an easier time of it." The rat jerked his thumb to the left.

Sassafras and Fuzzy followed his directions, and soon the three found themselves working their way down the shelving into the office. Fuzzy and Vinnie did, anyway; the parakeet just glided to the desktop.

"Show-off," whispered Vinnie.

Sassafras turned to them and bowed. "Don't hate me because I'm beautiful."

"Believe me," said the rat, landing on the desktop. "If I was gonna hate, beauty wouldn't be the reason."

Sassafras hop-fluttered her way along the counter to the tall metal filing cabinet standing beside it. "Here we go, gents."

"In there?" said Fuzzy, hopping down onto the counter. "Can't you just do your thing with the computer?" He nodded at the secretary's machine. Sassafras was always bragging about what a computer whiz she was.

"I would, but she already turned it off," said the bird.

"So?" said Vinnie. "Turn it back on."

She shook her head. "You don't get it. There's a password, and I don't know what it is. Luckily, they keep backups of some key records on paper."

Fuzzy regarded her. "How do you know all this?"

"Yeah," said Vinnie. "Ya been moonlightin' as a secretary?"

Sassafras cackled. "Hardly. Mrs. Martinez left me with Mrs. Gomez for a few days when they were working on a stinky science project in our classroom. I picked up a thing or two."

The bird flew to the top of the metal cabinet. "The file we need should be in the second drawer with the other student files. Can you get it open?"

"Ha!" said Vinnie. "Does a woodpecker hate a petrified forest?"

"Um, I guess?" said Fuzzy.

"Stand back and watch me work," said the rat.

But before he could begin his magic, the three pets started at the sound of a door closing down the hallway, followed by footsteps.

"Freeze!" whispered Fuzzy.

They held stock-still, Fuzzy and Vinnie on the counter, and Sassafras atop the filing cabinet. Not a feather fluttered, not a hair stirred. They might have been pet statues.

Seconds later, a human came into view. From the corner of his eye, Fuzzy recognized the sturdy, tank-like figure of Principal Flake trundling toward the exit door.

Uh-oh.

If the principal spotted pets roaming around school after hours, she wouldn't need any other excuse to ban them for good.

I am invisible, I am totally invisible, Fuzzy thought as hard as he could.

The principal's eyes were trained on the floor; her frown was deeper and darker than a coalminer's bath-water. Just before she reached the door, Mrs. Flake glanced absently over at the counter, then reached up to flip off the light switch.

All went dark.

Had she seen them? Fuzzy couldn't be sure.

Halfway out the door, the principal paused.

"Hide!" whispered Fuzzy, diving behind a potted plant.

On flickered the lights. Risking a glance behind him, Fuzzy saw that Vinnie had ducked behind the computer monitor and Sassafras had disappeared somewhere.

The silent pause seemed to stretch longer than a visit to the vet. Fuzzy's heartbeat thudded in his ears.

At last, Principal Flake gave a bemused snort. "Silly woman's got me seeing things," she muttered. Off went the lights. *Rattle-click* went the door lock.

The principal's heels *tok-tok-tok*ed down the corridor. The pets were alone once more.

"Whew!" said Sassafras, from somewhere behind the cabinet.

"You said it." Fuzzy slumped bonelessly to the countertop.

Vinnie's dim shape emerged from behind the computer monitor. "Enough lollygagging," he said. "Let's get crackin'."

Up onto a low shelf, then across to the filing cabinet he scrambled. Fuzzy followed. With a flutter of wings, Sassafras joined them. All three peered over the edge to the drawer handles below. Fuzzy's gut clenched. It was a sheer drop.

"Well?" said the bird. "What are you waiting for?"

"Don't rush me," said Vinnie. "I'm thinking."

Fuzzy backed away from the edge. "Can you, um, think faster?"

Arching an eyebrow, the rat said, "Feel free to pitch in. I'm not the only one here with a brain."

The pets examined the problem. "I know!" squawked Sassafras. "We could lower you by your tail."

"Nice try, Featherhead," said Vinnie. "No way I'm lettin' you two mooks pull off my favorite body part."

Fuzzy crept back to the edge and eyeballed the distance. "Wouldn't work, anyway. You'd need a tail as long as a kangaroo's."

They stared awhile longer.

"But ya could lower me with *somethin'*, that's for sure," said Vinnie. "They got any rope around here?"

"Let's find out," said Fuzzy.

Sassafras glided over to the desk and turned on a lamp to help illuminate the search. All three of them began poking into corners and cubbyholes around the office.

"Check this out!" squawked the bird, her nose in a deep drawer.

"What'd you find?" Fuzzy called.

"Mrs. Gomez has—*mmf*—a whole stash of fruit-flavored candy!" said Sassafras with her mouth full.

"Can ya tie it together into a rope?" asked Vinnie.

"*Mmf*, I doubt it," said the bird.

"Then keep searching."

Fuzzy unearthed stashes of pens, pencils, and Post-its, a bag of coffee beans, plant food, a brass bust of some guy with really long earlobes, back issues of some magazine called *Teachers' Universe*, and a box of stale Girl Scout Cookies. But no rope.

"Hey, hey," said Vinnie, half to himself.

"Whatcha got?" chirped Sassafras.

The rat held up a silver roll of what Fuzzy had heard humans call "duck tape," although nothing about it reminded him of an aquatic bird.

"The answer to our prayers," said Vinnie.

"It's not rope," said Fuzzy.

"But it'll do." Vinnie slung the roll over one shoulder and across his chest, like a desperado's bandolier. "Fellow pets, come lend me a paw."

CHAPTER 9

Duct Tape Dynasty

Working under the rat's direction, the three of them taped a long strip from the back to the front of the filing cabinet. Rather than tearing it off, though, Vinnie let the roll dangle off the edge.

"So we're taping the cabinet together?" said Sassafras.

In a flash, Fuzzy saw the rat's plan. "No, he's going to cling to the roll and lower himself."

"Got it in one, Chubby Cheeks," said Vinnie with a wink. "And you two won't even need to hold the other end."

The rat grinned, stepping off the top of the cabinet.

His feet went inside the roll, his paws gripped the edge of the tape, and he *push-push-push*ed with his feet.

With a cracking sound, it unrolled crookedly, maybe half an inch. Vinnie frowned. "Needs more weight."

Fuzzy gulped. It was a long way down to the floor, and guinea pigs weren't that great at gliding. But the rat needed his help—heck, all the pets needed his help. "Uh, coming," he said. Gripping the edge of tape tighter than an anaconda's hug, he gingerly stepped down inside the roll.

Crick-ack-ack-ack! Fuzzy and Vinnie jerked downward as the tape unspooled another few inches. *Yikes!* Fuzzy's stomach tried to escape through his throat. His eyes squeezed shut.

"That's the ticket!" cried Vinnie. "Again!"

Working together, Fuzzy and Vinnie unrolled their way down until both could stand on the second drawer's handle.

"What now?" Fuzzy asked, trying not to look down.

"A little hocus-pocus . . ." Reaching out with one foot, the rat pushed sideways on the button by the handle. When it clicked, he said, "Now put yer back against the cabinet and push with all yer might!"

Fuzzy followed instructions. When the drawer slid out with a *whoosh*, his heart lurched. *Whoomp!* Down plunked his guinea pig butt onto a wad of hanging files.

Vinnie smirked. "Grace personified."

Fuzzy shot him a look.

After a few more solid shoves, Fuzzy and Vinnie were able to push the drawer out far enough so they could rifle through the files.

"Is that Krumpton with a *C* or a *K*?" asked the rat.

"Not sure," said Fuzzy.

Sassafras stuck her head over the edge. "How's it going down there?"

"It'd go a whole lot faster with another pair of eyes," said Vinnie.

The bird joined them, balancing atop the hanging files as they flipped through the alphabet.

"Huh," said Sassafras after a minute.

"Find something?" asked Fuzzy.

"Yeah," said the bird. "Who knew that Mr. Chopra's kid went to kindergarten here?"

"Don't know, don't care," said Vinnie, flipping through folders. "Find the Krumpton."

"Righty-o."

In another minute, they had done just that. With a triumphant "a-ha!" Fuzzy plucked a file folder from the pack. He and Vinnie removed the first sheet and held it up to the light.

"Hey," said Sassafras, peering over their shoulders. "This Krumpton kid's in your class, Fuzzy."

"*My* class?" said Fuzzy.

It was true. Fuzzy hadn't learned all his students' last names yet, but there in black and white was *Abigail Krumpton, Room 5-B*. "Abby?" he said.

"Not the most memorable kid, huh?" said Sassafras.

"And she ain't much of a student, either," said the rat. "Check this out: straight C average."

Fuzzy shook his head. No wonder he didn't know Abby well enough to know her last name. She'd never been top student of the week, so she'd never taken him home for the weekend.

"Top student . . ." he mused.

"Right," said Vinnie. "In a bizzarro universe, maybe."

But Fuzzy scarcely heard him. He was staring off into space as the wheels of his brain ran round and round.

"I know that look," said Sassafras. "Fuzzy's about to have a brainstorm. Either that, or drop a load of piggy pellets—it's almost the same expression."

"Well?" said Vinnie. "Care to share?"

Fuzzy's gaze came down out of the clouds and focused on the rat's face. "We need to turn an average student into a top student in no time flat. Any ideas?"

Back in the pets' clubhouse, the group discussed Fuzzy's brainstorm with some skepticism.

"You want to turn Ava Average into Barbara Brainiac?" said Igor.

Mistletoe blinked. "I thought her name was Abby."

"Call her Prunella LaBoof if you like," said Igor. "Still can't be done."

"But she only has to be the best *this week*," said Fuzzy.

"And how do you suggest we do that?" said the iguana. "We can't exactly sit in on her study group."

Cinnabun batted her big brown eyes. "Dear Brother

Fuzzy, it's a lovely thought, truly. But I don't see how we can improve this girl's grades so quickly."

"Simple," said Luther. "Cheat."

Their bunny president put a paw to her chest. Her mouth dropped open. "Why, Brother Luther, I'm going to pretend you didn't say that."

"Lean, Long, and Legless has a point." Vinnie swaggered forward. "Our backs are up against the wall here. If we don't change this dame's mind toot sweet, she's gonna boot us out faster than you can spell *Pee Tee Ay*."

"*P-T-A*," said Mistletoe.

"That fast," said the rat. "I say desperate times call for desperate measures."

Fuzzy's tummy felt a little queasy. Cheating was wrong. But banning pets from school was even wrong-er.

He glanced around. Marta and Cinnabun looked the most scandalized by the idea, but the others seemed as though they were seriously considering it.

Sassafras spoke up. "Hang on, sports fans! Before we decide to go to the dark side, we need to know if there's something to cheat *on*. Does Fuzzy's class have a test this week?"

All eyes turned to Fuzzy.

"Well?" said Luther.

Fuzzy scratched his neck. "They, uh, do have a big history test tomorrow."

"There you go," said Vinnie. "Badda-bim, badda-boom. We give the girl an A-plus, and the Fuzzball goes home with her to spy and charm and change minds."

"Easy-peasy, baby," agreed Luther.

Fuzzy shifted uncomfortably. "I don't know . . ."

"What's the hang-up?" said Vinnie.

Marta pursed her lips. "His conscience, that's what."

Lifting a shoulder, Fuzzy said, "That, plus a few tricky bits."

"Like what?" asked Sassafras.

Fuzzy ticked off the challenges on his fingers. "Tricky Bit Number One: How do we get the test answers? Tricky Bit Number Two: How do we change Abby's test without Miss Wills knowing?"

"And Tricky Bit Number Three?" asked Igor.

"How do we live with ourselves afterward?" said Cinnabun.

Fuzzy winced. "I was going to say, if everything else works out and I do go home with Abby, how the heck do I change her mom's mind?"

Marta sighed. "That, my friend, is the trickiest bit of all."

CHAPTER 10

Cheater Pan

The choice was tougher than week-old cafeteria cube steak. But ultimately, the pets voted to cheat and remain at school, rather than be honorable and get kicked out. Cinnabun grumbled, but she went along with the majority.

Sassafras shook out her wings. "Now that that's settled, where do we find the test answers?"

The pets traded blank looks. None of them had ever had to get their paws on an answer key before.

"You don't know?" Fuzzy asked the parakeet. "You spent all that time in the office."

She shrugged. "It never came up."

"I thought Vinnie would know," said Mistletoe.

"Me?" said the rat. "Because I give so many tests, or because I'm basically dishonest?"

"Um, neither one?" said Mistletoe. "You just . . . know stuff."

He quirked an eyebrow. "Thanks, Short Stack. Fact is, I'm just as clueless as the rest of ya."

Fuzzy scratched his cheek, considering. "Seems to me that the test key would be in one of two places."

"Do tell," said Cinnabun.

"Either somewhere in the office, or in Miss Wills's desk."

The rabbit mulled this over. "Makes sense to me, y'all. What say we split into two teams and search both spots?"

Vinnie volunteered to lead the larger group into the office, since there was more ground to cover. Fuzzy took Mistletoe and Luther back to his classroom.

"After all, if three of us can't handle one desk," said the boa, "maybe we deserve to be kicked out."

By this time it was full dark, and the school had fallen as silent as a field mouse when a hawk's in the wind. Not that Fuzzy was afraid of the dark or anything, but he felt comforted by having his friends along. The more the merrier.

Climbing back down into Room 5-B was like descending into a gray whale's gullet. You couldn't see your paw in front of your face. Bumbling his way along by feel and smell, Fuzzy located Miss Wills's desk and turned on its lamp.

The room was bathed in a buttery-yellow glow. From the desktop beside him, Mistletoe surveyed Fuzzy's home. "Wow, nice place you got here," she said. "And such a roomy cage."

Fuzzy felt a bit embarrassed. "Guinea pigs need lots of space," he explained. "We're, um, restless."

"Of course," said the mouse.

Twining his way up the chair leg and into the seat, Luther scoped out their objective. "Looks like your standard, five-drawer teacher's desk. Piece of cake."

"Where?" Mistletoe looked about eagerly.

"Figure of speech, Little Bit," said the snake.

Fuzzy's chest felt tight. He couldn't help thinking how wrong this was. Miss Wills was his human. A pet shouldn't mess with his human's stuff or steal things from her.

But if he didn't do this, he might not be her class's pet for much longer. Fuzzy ground his teeth together. He hated tough decisions.

"So, what now?" Mistletoe asked, peering down at the boa.

Luther eyed the drawer just above him. "Join me, Fuzzarino?"

Fuzzy clambered down to the seat, with Mistletoe right behind him.

"Now, tug on that," the snake said, nodding at the drawer.

Stretching up on tiptoe, Fuzzy tried to pull it open. The drawer didn't budge. He tried the drawers to their right and left. Same result.

"Oh no," said Mistletoe.

The boa stayed as cool as a cucumber sandwich on ice. "Just as I suspected," he said. "Your teacher locks up after herself."

"And she takes her keys home with her," said Fuzzy. "*Now* how do we get into the desk?"

Luther grinned. "Old-fashioned ingenuity, baby," he said. "Tell me, where might a reptile find a paper clip?" When Fuzzy pointed to the desktop, the boa glided up there, rustled through some papers, and returned with the item in his mouth.

"*Mmfa umfo mfss?*" he asked.

Fuzzy and Mistletoe exchanged a glance and a shrug. Spitting the paper clip onto the seat, Luther repeated, "Can you unfold thi*sss*?"

The mouse brightened. "Why didn't you say so? Posi-tutely!" She and Fuzzy gripped the metal clasp, pulling and twisting until one end of the loop had straightened out.

"That'll do," said Luther. He wriggled upward until his midsection was resting on the chair arm. Then he put his lips to the lock's keyhole, hawked up a loogie, and spat.

"Eeww," said Mistletoe.

"Does snake spit melt locks?" asked Fuzzy.

"Wouldn't that be cool?" said the boa. "But nah, the mechanism's gotta be lubricated." He asked for the paper clip, and Fuzzy passed it up to him. Taking the looped end in his mouth, Luther stuck the straightened end into the keyhole, and, eyes half shut, began jiggering it around.

"This is exciting," said Mistletoe.

"Yup," said Fuzzy, eyes on Luther.

"Kind of like a heist movie," said Mistletoe.

"Uh-huh."

"When do you think he'll be done?"

Luther shot them a sidelong glance. *"Fmfuh umfo mm ggh."*

"I think he said, 'Sooner, if you don't talk,'" said Fuzzy.

The mouse flashed an embarrassed smile and pantomimed zipping her lips.

Shuffling from foot to foot, Fuzzy watched as the snake fiddled with the lock. Could Luther really pick it like a master burglar, or had he just watched too many crime movies?

At long last, something went *click*, and Luther mumbled, *"Mmf umg muh."*

"Let me guess," Mistletoe squeaked. "'Hawk another loogie?'"

The snake rolled his eyes.

Fuzzy smothered a smile. "I think maybe he wants us to try tugging." Stretching as high as he could, Fuzzy pulled back on the underside of the drawer with all his might.

Schoof! It slid out smoothly and quickly—too quickly.

Boof! Fuzzy landed on his bottom.

Helping him up, Mistletoe said, "Do we search the drawer now?"

"Let's," said Fuzzy. While Luther picked the other two locks, he and Mistletoe rummaged through the random collection of junk in the center drawer.

The scissors, stapler, pencils, and office supplies held no surprises. Nor did the random toys, games, and other items confiscated from students. All these were expected. But where were the test answers?

As soon as Luther cracked the lock on the left, Fuzzy and Mistletoe moved on to search the top drawer below it.

"This looks more like it," said the mouse, flipping through file folders. "Check this out: attendance records . . . field trips . . . ooh, complaints!"

"We shouldn't . . ." Fuzzy began.

But the mouse had already tugged the folder free and was pulling papers from it. "Aren't you curious? Let's see if there're any complaints about you!"

Intrigued despite himself, Fuzzy scanned the top sheet, written in the teacher's graceful cursive. Luther's head peeked over his shoulder.

"There you are, Fuzzrod," he said, reading from the sheet. "Looks like you chirp during test time."

"Only when I'm excited," said Fuzzy.

"And you pooped on a student's hand?" Mistletoe giggled.

"Not my fault," Fuzzy protested. "He startled me."

Luther squinted at the paper. "Whoa, baby," he said. "This is the *sss*erious stuff."

Mistletoe read the entry aloud:

94

"Mrs. Summers complained that guinea pig caused an accident while home for the weekend with Malik. Student was injured. Mother requested that he no longer bring guinea pig home to pet-sit."

The other two pets stared at Fuzzy.

"Didn't you say Malik's mom was a friend of the PTA president?" said Mistletoe.

"Um, yeah," said Fuzzy, studying the floor.

"And now this Krumpton woman is trying to ban all pets?" said Luther.

"Yeah . . ."

"Are these things somehow . . . connected?" asked Luther.

Fuzzy's ears felt warmer than a car seat in the summer sun. "It was all a, um, misunderstanding," he squeaked. Fuzzy *really* didn't want his friends to know that his goof at Malik's house had led to their current predicament. "Blown out of proportion."

"Is that so?" said Luther mildly.

Fuzzy couldn't take it anymore. "Okay, okay, it's all my fault!" he cried. "I made a kid trip, he hit Malik, and now that lady wants to kick us all out. I'm so, so sorry!"

The other two pets were silent for a beat. Then Mistletoe rested a paw on his shoulder. "It was an accident," she said. "Everybody has accidents."

Fuzzy hung his head. "I'm a bad pet."

"I'll say." Luther smirked. "Our Fuzzy's been a naughty, naughty piggy."

"But we're still your friends," said Mistletoe. "Right, Luther?"

"Sure thing," said Luther, sliding the sheet back into its folder. "You bad boy, you."

Despite wanting to melt into the floor, Fuzzy was relieved to have everything out in the open at last. He was truly a lucky rodent to have friends like these.

"Can we, um, get back to searching now?" he asked.

The others agreed, and soon their hunt was rewarded. In the next drawer down, the pets found exactly what they were looking for.

"Jackpot!" squeaked Mistletoe.

The other two crowded close as the mouse worked the history tests folder out from among the other files. "Careful," said Fuzzy. "Don't tear it or anything."

Flipping through the test sheets, they located the one with Tuesday's date. As he stared at it, Fuzzy shivered involuntarily. He'd never done anything this illegal before.

"We're in luck," said Luther. "It's mostly a multiple-choice test. Just one essssay question."

Fuzzy made a face. "An essay? Uh-oh. No way can we imitate Abby's handwriting well enough to fool Miss Wills."

"Then let's hope that the multiple-choice part is enough," said the snake. "So how do you want to work this?"

"What do you mean?" asked Fuzzy, thinking that he'd rather not be working it at all.

"You can't just steal the sheet, because your teacher would miss it," said Luther.

"Duh," said Mistletoe. "Even I know that."

Fuzzy's forehead wrinkled in thought. "I guess we write down the answers on a little slip of paper."

"Yeah, I figured that," said Luther. "I meant, do we hide the answers in your girl's desk so she can find it, or do you want to change her answers afterward?"

Fuzzy considered the options. He couldn't count on Abby discovering the cheat sheet—in fact, the way things were going, Miss Wills would find it first.

"I'll change them afterward."

"All righty, then!" said the mouse. She scrambled up to the desktop and lifted a pen from a mug full of writing utensils. "You call 'em out, I'll write 'em down."

Taking turns, Luther and Fuzzy read the test answers aloud while Mistletoe scribbled. Afterward, Fuzzy made sure to double-check her cheat sheet against the test key. It wasn't that he didn't trust her; it's just that she was . . . Mistletoe. Things happened without her meaning them to.

When the three pets had closed all the drawers and restored everything to how it used to be, Luther and Mistletoe headed home to their own classrooms. The mouse volunteered to tell the other pets to call off their search. After they'd gone, Fuzzy buried his cheat sheet under the pine shavings that lined the floor of his habitat. He tried to sleep.

Lying there in the dark, he could almost feel the stolen test answers, radiating heat like a sore tooth. Fuzzy tossed and turned, trying to ease his conscience.

He didn't see any other way out of the spot the pets were in. But as he fought for sleep, he had to wonder: Would this desperate move be enough to save them?

CHAPTER 11

Testing, One, Two

As it turned out, a troubled conscience made for just as restful a sleep as napping on a bed of nails. Bleary-eyed, Fuzzy awoke the next morning to the sound of Miss Wills's key in the lock.

For a moment or two, it felt like any other groggy morning after a sleepless night. And then he remembered.

Wheek! Fuzzy shot bolt upright, banging his head on the ceiling of his igloo. Scurrying outside, he scanned his cage for evidence of last night's caper. There! A corner of his cheat sheet peeked out from under the pine shavings.

Wiggling whiskers!

He dove across the cage to block it from his teacher's sight.

"What's gotten into you, big guy?" asked Miss Wills, heading for her desk. "Did you have jumping beans for breakfast?"

With elaborate casualness, Fuzzy kicked some pine shavings over the slip of paper, hiding it from view. He watched as Miss Wills set down her bag, hung her sweater over the back of her chair, and unlocked her desk.

Would she notice any sign of their tampering?

The teacher frowned slightly as she opened the second lock, the one Luther had had the hardest time re-engaging.

Just then, the classroom phone rang. With a final glance at the desk, Miss Wills set down her key ring and went to answer the call.

"Yes . . . ? Oh, I see," she said. "And when is—? Okay . . . okay, I will."

By the time she'd hung up, Miss Wills's expression had turned serious. Fortunately, Fuzzy noticed, she seemed to have forgotten all about the locks on her desk.

"Miss Wills, Miss Wills!" Two students, Maya and Natalia, burst through the door.

"What is it, girls?" asked the teacher.

They hurried up to her desk, book bags still swinging from their shoulders. "We heard there's going to be some big meeting on Monday about getting rid of pets," said Maya.

Fuzzy crossed his cage and gripped the bars. Mrs. Krumpton had followed through on her threat already? His throat went drier than a ditch digger in the Sahara Desert.

"They can't really do that, can they?" asked Natalia, pushing her enormous glasses up the bridge of her nose.

"You girls are well informed." Miss Wills raised her eyebrows. "I just heard about it myself."

"You won't let them kick Fuzzy out, will you?" asked Maya.

"It's not right," added Natalia. Several students who'd just walked in echoed her complaint.

The teacher held up a palm. "I agree. It's a terrible idea to get rid of our classroom pets, and I'll certainly speak against it at the meeting. But the decision's not up to me."

Natalia pouted. "Why not?"

Smoothing the girl's hair off her forehead, Miss Wills said, "Honey, in our country, the majority rules—even when we don't like the choices it makes."

"That's not fair," said Natalia.

Miss Wills gave a wry smile. "Tell me about it."

More and more kids trickled into the classroom, but Fuzzy scarcely noticed. His attention was riveted to the conversation.

"But won't the principal stop this from happening?" asked Malik, sitting down.

"Mrs. Flake's power isn't absolute," said the teacher. "If the whole school votes to ban pets, there's not much she can do."

"So we've got to make sure the school votes the right way." Maya's eyes narrowed. "They're not getting rid of Fuzzy without a fight."

"Yeah," said Heavy-Handed Jake, joining them. "There's got to be something we can do."

Fuzzy's heart lifted at all this support from his students. But he wondered what they could actually accomplish in just a few short days.

Miss Wills surveyed the group. "You want to do something?"

"Yeah!" they chorused.

"Then testify at that meeting that you like having a pet in the classroom."

"But can't we do something more?" Fuzzy was surprised to see that it was Abby who'd spoken up.

Miss Wills considered for a moment. "Well, I suppose you could try to influence the rest of the students and their parents."

"You mean by telling them how awesome pets are?" said Malik.

"Or collecting signatures on a petition?" asked Abby.

"Exactly," said the teacher as the morning bell rang. She motioned to the students to take their seats.

Abby nodded and obeyed, her expression thoughtful. Even though Fuzzy now knew who her mom was, he couldn't quite picture it. The two were nothing alike. Where Mrs. Krumpton was tall, blonde, and bossy, her daughter was short and quiet with mousy-brown pigtails.

But her heart was in the right place.

Fuzzy hoped his plan to go home with her would succeed. Even more, he hoped it wouldn't land her in trouble.

All through science and English lessons, Fuzzy fussed and fidgeted. Now that cheating time was at hand, he couldn't sit still.

Shortly before lunch, Miss Wills told the students to put away their books and break out their number two pencils. "And now, the moment you've all been dreaming of," she said. "Our history test."

Mixed groans and chuckles greeted her remark.

As she stowed her textbook in her desk, Abby sighed, grimacing at the girl next to her. This didn't give Fuzzy a lot of confidence in her test-taking abilities. But luckily, he could help with that.

In an agony of impatience, Fuzzy only just restrained himself from chirping during the test. He climbed up and down his platform, gnawed on his block, and circled his habitat. It seemed like a month of Mondays had passed by the time Miss Wills told the kids to put down their pencils and pass their tests forward.

As the teacher was collecting their papers, the lunch bell rang. She told the students to go on ahead to the cafeteria.

Fuzzy watched closely while she gathered all the tests into a red folder and slipped that file into the center desk drawer. *Don't lock it, don't lock it,* he silently pleaded. And for once, his prayers were answered.

Miss Wills headed out for her own lunch without locking anything. Her desk was left wide open to intrepid rodents.

As soon as the door closed behind her, Fuzzy shoved his platform, ball, and blocks into escape position. He didn't know exactly how long she'd be gone, so he had to hurry.

Unfortunately, he hurried so much that he was nearly out of the cage before he remembered his hidden answer sheet. *Duh.* Fuzzy pulled his whiskers, then hopped back down to retrieve the test key.

Folding it carefully and holding the slip in his mouth, Fuzzy retraced his steps. Up and over he went, landing on the table with an *oof!*

So far, so good.

Moving as quickly as the last days of summer vacation, Fuzzy slid down to the floor and hurried across to Miss Wills's desk. He'd already eaten up five minutes. No time to waste.

Up he scrambled onto the chair, then the desktop. Leaning over the edge, Fuzzy slid out the center drawer. There lay the red folder, right on top.

Just as he reached for it, something clattered against the door. He froze.

Should he hide, or wait it out? In an agony of indecision, Fuzzy stared at the door, eyes riveted and hackles bristling.

No further sounds followed. His hammering heartbeat gradually slowed, and Fuzzy decided that someone must have bumped the door on their way down the hall. He reached down and lifted the folder onto the desk.

Time to—

Too late, Fuzzy realized he'd kept the test answers in his mouth this entire time. He spat out the folded slip of paper and gasped. There were bite marks on it.

Suffering mange mites!

With trembling paws, Fuzzy unfolded the test key. Were the answers still readable?

He ran down the list. Nearly all the solutions were intact, except for three that had been marred by his bite. Fuzzy checked the clock. No time to dig out the teacher's answer sheet again. His imperfect list would have to do.

Separating Abby's history test from the rest, he laid it on the desktop beside his cheat sheet. *Yeesh*. Nearly half of the girl's answers were wrong. Fuzzy was no brainiac, but clearly someone needed to spend less time with video games and more time with textbooks.

Snagging a pencil from the mug, he erased Abby's first mistake, filling in the correct answer.

Fuzzy gasped again.

His writing was in red. He'd grabbed the wrong pencil!

Erasing furiously, Fuzzy rewrote the answer with a regular number two pencil. This time, it looked right.

He blew out a sigh. This cheating stuff was harder than it looked.

Fuzzy worked his way down Abby's test sheet, laboriously erasing and correcting as he went. The minutes ticked past, as fast as a falcon's dive. By the time Fuzzy had finished up, only five minutes remained in lunch period.

After a last quick check of his answers, Fuzzy blew away the eraser shavings and slipped Abby's test into the red folder. Back into the drawer it went.

Well, that's that, he thought, preparing to jump down onto the seat. But Fuzzy paused with one paw dangling in space. He couldn't squelch the nagging feeling that he'd overlooked something.

But what?

Scanning the desktop one last time, Fuzzy gave a *wheek!* His cheat sheet! There it lay, right out in plain sight where Miss Wills was sure to spot it.

Careless guinea pig! That would be all he—or Abby—needed, for the teacher to discover the cheat sheet. Fuzzy snatched up the slip of paper, tucked it into his cheek, and scrambled down to the floor.

Whew. As he crossed the room and scaled the table that held his habitat, Fuzzy began to relax. He'd gotten away with it. And then, just as he was scaling his cage wall, Fuzzy heard something: the clatter of a key in the lock!

Adrenaline blasted through his veins. With a burst of speed, he scrambled the rest of the way up and flopped over the cage wall onto his platform.

Safe.

The door swung open. In strolled Miss Wills with Maya by her side. The teacher glanced his way. "Were your ears burning, big guy? We were just talking about you."

"Hey, what's that in his mouth?" asked Maya.

Fuzzy jumped.

Oops. He'd forgotten to hide the evidence!

CHAPTER 12

Bambi Eyes

Burning with guilt, Fuzzy *chew-chew-chew*ed up the cheat sheet. The closer Maya and Miss Wills came, the faster he chomped. By the time they reached Fuzzy's habitat, the last of the paper had vanished.

Gulp.

Fuzzy gazed up at them with as much innocence as he could muster. It wasn't much.

Miss Wills studied him with her head at an angle. "Well, whatever it was, it's in his belly now."

"I just hope it doesn't disagree with him," said Maya.

Fuzzy nearly barfed the pulpy paper back out. The whole *idea* of cheating disagreed with him. But sometimes a rodent's gotta do what a rodent's gotta do.

Luckily, Miss Wills and Maya walked away without noticing that Fuzzy had set up his cage for escape. He clambered down to the pine shavings and quietly pushed apart his ball and blocks.

That had been *way* too close for comfort. It would take a long nap and a short snack before Fuzzy felt like himself again.

In the clubhouse after school, the other pets crowded around, peppering Fuzzy with questions.

"Did you find Abby's test?" asked Mistletoe.

"Did anyone catch ya?" asked Vinnie.

"How's the life of crime, you cheater-cheater-pumpkin-eater?" Igor sneered.

Holding up his palms, Fuzzy said, "Whoa, slow down!"

Cinnabun rested her paw on his shoulder. "Mission accomplished, Brother Fuzzy?"

"I think so," he said.

As his friends surrounded him, Fuzzy filled them in on his eventful morning, on the upcoming school meeting, and on his first experience as a cheater. When he finished, the others still had concerns.

"But suppose somebody gets a better grade than Abby?" asked Mistletoe. "What then?"

With a shrug, Fuzzy said, "I guess we try to figure out a plan B."

"We better plan fast if the meeting is Monday," said Luther.

Mistletoe shook her head. "I still can't believe the kids and teachers might really kick us out. After all we've meant to them? So sad."

"Some of them are definitely on our side," said Fuzzy. "My students are planning to testify for us."

Vinnie grinned. "And somebody's been putting up pro-pet posters. We saw two of 'em in the office when we searched yesterday."

"And I *sss*potted one in the hallway," said Luther. "Mysterious benefactors, baby."

Sassafras hopped from foot to foot. "Never mind that—when will we know Abby's grade? The suspense is killing me!"

"By Thursday afternoon," said Fuzzy. "Or Friday morning at the latest. That's when Miss Wills usually announces the week's top student."

Igor clasped a paw to his chest. "Ugh. I'm getting indigestion from waiting."

"Sure that's not from eating?" said Vinnie. "I noticed those stale Girl Scout Cookies went missing."

The iguana stuck out his tongue at him.

Jumping up onto the presidential podium, Cinnabun raised her paws. "Settle down, y'all. I've got the perfect way to pass the time."

"What, tiddlywinks?" scoffed Vinnie, under his breath.

"Cuteness lessons," said the rabbit, and she clasped her paws together adorably.

"Eh?" said Luther.

"Yay!" said Mistletoe.

"No way," said Fuzzy.

The rabbit surveyed the group. "If Brother Fuzzy is fixin' to charm our dear Mrs. Krumpton into changing her mind, he'll need a little help."

"He'll need a *lot* of help," said Igor.

Vinnie squinted skeptically. "And who's gonna lead this charm school?"

"Why, *moi*, of course," said Cinnabun.

Fuzzy slumped, shaking his head. When the rabbit got on a cuteness kick, not even the US Marines, King Kong, and the Green Bay Packers together could stop her.

Mistletoe applauded. "Fantabulous idea!"

Igor and Vinnie traded a look. "This oughta be rich," Vinnie muttered.

"And I trust you'll do the exercises too, for solidarity," said Cinnabun.

The rat's eyes popped. "But—"

"Bless your heart, Brother Vinnie!" said Cinnabun. "And all of y'all will take part too?"

The other pets bobbed their heads. What else could they do?

"Then let's begin," said Cinnabun. "Lesson Number One: Bambi Eyes."

Igor frowned. "What's that?"

Dimples sprouted on the rabbit's cheeks. "Why, only the most basic tool in the cuteness toolbox. Say, for example, you accidentally mess in your human's bed or break some treasured knickknack. They pitch a hissy fit. What do you do?"

"Hide in my shell?" said Marta.

"Stare 'em down," said Luther.

"Run," said Mistletoe.

Indulgently, Cinnabun shook her head. "Bless your pea-pickin' hearts. No, no, and no. You do . . . *this*." She ducked her head momentarily and looked up again, her caramel eyes huge, dewy, and almost painfully cute. When she batted them, her audience melted.

"Awww," said most of the pets in the room. Even Vinnie was struck dumb. Fuzzy had to admit, Cinnabun knew adorable like Inuits know snow.

"Simple, but powerful," said the rabbit, returning to her normal expression (which was still pretty darned cute). "Now you, Brother Fuzzy."

Heaving a sigh, Fuzzy tried to follow her example. He dropped his head, then whipped it up fast, eyes open wide.

"Were you fixin' to act scared?" said Cinnabun.

Vinnie snorted. "Looks like he just heard there's a hay shortage."

"Oh, ha-ha," said Fuzzy.

"Try again," said Cinnabun. "Only this time, make your eyes softer than a baby duck's belly. Brother Vinnie, why don't you join him?"

"Me?" said the rat.

"Why, yes."

Fuzzy and Vinnie tried the move, with varying degrees of success.

"Brother Vinnie, your eyes tell me you're sleepy," said the rabbit. "Try adding some more sugar to your gaze." She surveyed the rest of the group. "All of y'all, join in, now."

Fuzzy sent up a silent prayer and got ready to try Bambi Eyes again. *The things I do for the good of this club,* he thought.

CHAPTER 13

Winner and a Movie

When you're waiting to hear about something that will affect your whole life, every minute seems like a week, and every hour like a year. By the time Miss Wills made her announcement on Friday morning, Fuzzy felt old enough to be his own great-grandfather.

He sat up straight, electrified, when at last he heard Miss Wills say, "Time to announce the top student of the week. Attention, everyone!"

The boys and girls of 5-B leaned forward, focusing on her words.

"Our newest student-of-the-week winner has never

won before," said the teacher. "And I'm very proud of her for how much she's improved."

Her? thought Fuzzy. *That's promising.*

"She'll get to enjoy two whole days of pet-sitting our class mascot, Fuzzy," said Miss Wills, a smile tugging the corners of her lips. "And now, drumroll, please!"

All the students pounded their hands on their thighs, and the classroom echoed with, *Tuppa-tuppa-tuppa-tuppa-tuppa!*

"The top student for this week is . . . Abigail Krumpton!"

The thigh thumping turned to scattered applause. Abby's jaw dropped, her hands flew to her face, and she fell back in her chair. She looked as stunned as a mullet that just met a mallet.

Fuzzy knew what she was feeling, because he felt it too. Then, after the shock wore off, excitement set in: He was going home with Abby that afternoon!

Wheek, wheek! Fuzzy popcorned, bouncing up and down like a rodent pogo stick, and stirring up miniature explosions of pine shavings.

Kids laughed. "Hey, I think maybe Fuzzy likes the idea!" bellowed Loud Brandon.

After the class settled down again, Miss Wills steered her students back to discussing centimeters and inches and all things measurement-related. The whole time, that wide, incredulous smile never left Abby's face.

Fuzzy's heart melted for her. The poor girl had never been singled out as a good student, never had the privilege of pet-sitting him. He felt his own grin stretch wider just watching her.

If it took a bit of creative cheating to bring that smile to her face, Fuzzy wasn't at all sorry. (Well, maybe a teensy bit, but he tried to ignore it.) They would have great fun together, he and Abby. Moreover, Mrs. Krumpton would see that having a pet was a good thing, something to be encouraged, not denied.

At lunchtime, Abby asked Miss Wills for permission to take a photo of Fuzzy. "It's for my testimony on Monday," she said.

"I'm sure he won't mind," said the teacher.

Fuzzy happily posed for a shot. Heck, he'd wear a Little Bo-Peep outfit and dance the mambo if she'd asked, so thrilled and relieved was he that the pets' plan was moving forward.

The end of the day couldn't come soon enough for Fuzzy. After a short forever, the final bell rang, and Miss Wills dismissed her students for the weekend. Working with Abby, she transferred Fuzzy to his pet carrier. She handed the girl a bag full of instructions, food, and a few toys.

Before letting Abby go, Miss Wills asked, "Now, your mother knows about this, right? And she approves?"

"Oh, um, absolutely," said Abby. "Mom is totally up for it."

"But I thought she wasn't that crazy about pets," said Miss Wills.

Abby's smile looked a little strained. "Uh, just in the classroom," she said. "Mom's fine with pets at home."

"All right, then," said Miss Wills. "Have fun with Fuzzy, and I'll see you on Monday."

Loading herself up with her book bag, the pet-care bag, and Fuzzy's travel cage, Abby tottered out the doorway and into the hall. "See ya!" she called back.

The school bubbled and fizzed like a shaken-up soda. All around them percolated that special kind of enthusiasm that only comes on a Friday afternoon. Kids chattered about their weekend plans, hooted and ran about, and generally celebrated having two days off.

Slowly and steadily, Abby forged through the crowd. Just before exiting the front door, she stopped to remove a T-shirt from her book bag and drape it over the top of the carrier. Now Fuzzy couldn't see out.

"Hey!" he cried.

"It won't be for long," she told him. "We just need to keep things undercover for a little while."

Fuzzy naturally assumed the other kids would be jealous of her good fortune, so he could appreciate her wanting to keep him incognito. He settled onto the floor of his carrier and enjoyed the girl-sweat scent emanating from the T-shirt.

The carrier swayed as Abby pushed through the door and descended the steps. Would they travel by bus or by foot, Fuzzy wondered? He doubted that they'd walk home, since the girl seemed so overburdened.

Sure enough, the sharp stink of gasoline grew stronger, and the slam of car doors barked around them. Fuzzy felt the carrier being set down. A car door creaked open.

"Why so much gear, sweetie?" came a familiar female voice. Mrs. Krumpton, Fuzzy realized.

"Oh, just some school projects, Mom," said Abby.

"That's nice. Oh, what a day I've had!"

Up flew the carrier, settling onto a comfortable seat. The piney tang of air freshener mixed with the vehicle's new-car smell. As Fuzzy took a deep whiff, he could tell that not a latte had been spilled in this car, nor a french fry dropped.

Mrs. Krumpton pulled away from the curb, yammering about house showings and other real estate business. On and on she went, barely pausing to draw breath. Not once did she ask about her daughter's day at school. After about five minutes of this monologue, Fuzzy felt no closer to changing the PTA president's mind. *Patience*, he told himself. *Rome wasn't charmed in a day.*

As the ride wore on, Fuzzy realized that Abby hadn't mentioned him. Odd. For most of his students, the first thing out of their mouths would have been, "Hey, Mom, I'm pet-sitting Fuzzy." But not Abby.

At last, the car bumped over a dip and pulled to a stop. Doors popped open. "Here, let me take that," said Abby's mother. "You're carrying too much already."

"I've got it, Mom," said the girl.

"It's really no problem, sweetie. Let me."

"I can carry it myself."

Something jostled the carrier. For a few moments, it jerked this way and that, like the world's worst carnival ride. Fuzzy braced his feet on the floor. Were Abby and her mother fighting over who would lug him around?

"I *said* I've got it," said Abby.

"Oh-*kay*." Mrs. Krumpton sounded slightly offended. "Far be it from your old mom to try to lighten your load."

Rising off the seat, the carrier swung outside into fresh air. Fuzzy could sense the girl rearranging all her bags. Then, *scrunch-scrunch-scrunch,* they marched up what sounded like a gravel path, across some flagstones, and into an echoing entryway.

"I'll make up a snack for you," said Mrs. Krumpton. "How about that, Abs?"

"I'm not hungry," said Abby.

Fuzzy heard the random thumps of items being set down on a table. "It won't take me but a minute. Good nutrition is the key to healthy brain development, and we want to make sure you have every advantage. Yes, we do." The PTA president's voice receded as her heels clicked away, presumably toward the kitchen.

"Come on, Fuzzy," said Abby. "We're going to my room."

The lemony scent of furniture polish made Fuzzy's nose twitch as the carrier swayed its way along through several rooms. *How big is this house?* Fuzzy wondered.

Finally, they entered a chamber that smelled like strawberries. A door closed behind them. The carrier landed on a soft surface, and the T-shirt was whisked away. Fuzzy found himself on a wide bed at the center of a cozy bedroom. The space was decorated with oodles of pillows, posters of female astronauts and scientists, and fluffy clouds painted on robin's-egg-blue walls.

"I still can't believe I was top student," said Abby, setting down the pet-care bag. "Oh, Fuzzy, we'll have so much fun together!"

Fuzzy blinked. For someone who rarely said much during school hours, Abby was turning out to be just as chatty as her classmates. He wondered if it was a relief for her to talk to someone who only listened.

Fuzzy shook himself. Human behavior was fascinating, but it was way beyond him. He needed to stretch his legs and explore. Fuzzy scratched at his carrier walls.

"Want to see my room?" asked Abby. "Hang on." Opening the top of the portable cage, she lifted him out and set him on the bed.

Much better. Fuzzy scampered about, testing pillows and sniffing the oversized panda-bear toy. Abby laughed in delight. "Fuzzy, this is Chi Chi. He's so pleased to meet you."

Suddenly, the door swung open. "Here we go," chirped Mrs. Krumpton. "Some cucumber sandwiches and apple slices with—*aaugh!*" she cried, catching sight of Fuzzy. "What the heck is *that*?"

CHAPTER 14

Home, Home, and Deranged

Abby sprang to her feet, stepping between her mother and the bed. "This is Fuzzy, our class pet."

The woman's mouth dropped open in a perfect O. "The same one that almost gave a concussion to Shondra's boy? What in the world is it doing here?"

In her shock, Mrs. Krumpton let the plate tilt, threatening to dump the cucumber sandwiches on the floor. Though keenly aware of the threat that Abby's mom posed, Fuzzy couldn't help thinking that he'd be happy to clean up any cucumber slices that fell.

"I was the top student in class this week," said Abby. "So I got to take him home."

"This awful creature that caused so much trouble?" said Mrs. Krumpton. "Honestly, I can't believe you'd be so insensitive."

"But it's—"

"This thing is a menace. How could you even think of . . ." Belatedly, Abby's mother realized that her daughter had done well academically. "Of course I'm proud that you got a good grade, sweetie. But really, after all the fuss I've been making over Malik's accident? After my campaign to protect you kids from pets? How could you do this to me?"

Abby's lower lip trembled, but she stood her ground. "You're always on me to get better grades."

"Yes, because—"

"Well, I finally did. Why won't you let me enjoy this?"

Mrs. Krumpton opened her mouth to speak, thought better of it, and then set the plate on the bed. Fuzzy eyed the sandwiches.

"Abs, I'm glad that you did well," said the woman, her voice softening. "I've always said you're smart enough to get top grades if you just apply yourself."

Abby rolled her eyes.

"But there are better ways to celebrate your success," said her mother. "Now, call up your teacher and ask her to take this . . . thing away."

The girl ducked her head, and her lips thinned to a tight line. "I can't," she squeaked.

"I'll call her for you, then. What's her number?"

"Miss Wills is, um, away for the weekend," said Abby. Fuzzy shot her a glance. This was the first he'd heard of it. "She's gone, and I promised to take care of Fuzzy."

"Oh, come now. There must be someone else you could leave it with," said Mrs. Krumpton. "Let's call them right now."

Let's not, thought Fuzzy. It wouldn't help his plans at all.

"No," said Abby, lifting her chin. "Fuzzy's my responsibility, and I have to take care of him."

The little muscles in Mrs. Krumpton's cheeks jumped as she ground her teeth together. "You agreed to this without even consulting me?"

"Please, Mom? You never let me have a dog or a cat, not even a hamster."

"That's for your own good, sweetie," said Abby's mother. "You know that. We've been over this before."

Abby's face formed an expression that Fuzzy thought might be the human version of Bambi Eyes. *"Pleeease,* Mom? It's just for two days."

The PTA president drew in a long breath and pursed her lips. She tilted her head, looking from her daughter to Fuzzy. And then she exhaled.

"Oh, all right," said Mrs. Krumpton grudgingly.

"Yay!" squealed Abby.

Her mother held up a warning finger. "But just for this weekend, and only in certain parts of the house. I want that thing closely supervised. No repeats of what happened to Malik."

"Thanks, Mom." Abby gave her mother a quick hug.

"And you've got to feed it and clean up its messes," said her mother.

With a hand on her heart, Abby said, "Of course. That's exactly what I promised Miss Wills, anyway."

Folding her arms, Mrs. Krumpton sent Fuzzy a dubious look. "Don't make me regret this."

"I won't," Abby vowed.

Eyes narrowed, Mrs. Krumpton turned and swept from the room. Watching her go, Fuzzy thought, *Getting in was easy. Charming Ms. Personality will be a whole other ball of wax.*

Fuzzy didn't see much of Mrs. Krumpton that afternoon. The woman's voice droned from a nearby room as she made phone call after work-related phone call. Meanwhile, Abby let Fuzzy explore her bedroom. He was glad she didn't have other pets for him to contend with, but he wondered when he'd get the chance to curry favor with her mother.

It didn't come that night. Or the next day. On Sunday, Abby and her mother left the house for a long stretch, and when they returned, the girl was limping and in tears.

She flopped on the bed, hugging a pillow. Lying there in her electric-yellow shirt, teal shorts, and high socks, Abby looked like some kind of athlete. But her eyes leaked like a faucet fixed by a cut-rate plumber.

Fuzzy's heart went out to her. From his carrier on the table, he whined sympathetically.

Abby raised her head. Wiping her eyes, she got up, fetched Fuzzy, and carried him back to the bed. He nuzzled her under the chin.

That set off a fresh round of waterworks. "Oh, Fuzzy," she moaned. "I just hate soccer so much."

Climbing from her embrace up onto her shoulder, Fuzzy licked her cheek. Abby giggled through her tears. She took him in her arms again and cuddled him.

"Sometimes it feels like you're the only one who gets me," she said.

"That's my job," he chirped, snuggling closer.

Eventually, the tears dried up, and Fuzzy was able to guide her into a healthy round of play to take her mind off things. By dinnertime, she was acting much more chipper.

Fuzzy still wasn't allowed to eat with the family. Left alone in his carrier, he munched his hay and fresh veggies, wondering when he'd get his opportunity with Mrs. Krumpton. All afternoon, he'd done his best to comfort Abby, but unless her mother witnessed their closeness, it wouldn't help his mission.

Finally, his chance came. After dinner, Abby and her mother retired to the TV room, and the girl brought Fuzzy along. Like the rest of the house, this chamber was immaculate. A champagne-colored couch and armchairs faced a widescreen TV playing some silly detective show.

Abby plopped down on the sofa with Fuzzy, while her mother sat in the chair with her computer tablet. Right away, Fuzzy assumed a snuggling position on Abby's lap. The girl stroked his fur absently while watching the show. He purred.

From time to time, Mrs. Krumpton looked up from her tablet to the TV. She completely ignored Fuzzy.

He frowned. This wouldn't do. Time to crank things up a notch.

Leaving Abby's lap, Fuzzy scrambled up the sofa arm and along the top of the cushions. Stepping down onto the girl's shoulder, he nuzzled into her neck.

"Hee-hee, that tickles!" Abby said.

From the corner of his eye, Fuzzy noticed Mrs. Krumpton glancing their way. He gave the girl an extra-affectionate snuggle and a lick.

Abby broke into giggles. "Aw, you're sweet."

"Don't let that thing lick you," said Mrs. Krumpton. "Who knows what diseases you might catch?"

"Mr. Wong just checked him out," said Abby. "Fuzzy's fine."

Her mother made a face like she'd bitten into a toffee and found it full of earwax. "They're all riddled with disease; it's a well-known fact," she said. Then Mrs. Krumpton returned her attention to her tablet.

Fuzzy grimaced. Was this woman's heart made of stone? What would it take to win her over?

Treating Abby's arm like a slide, Fuzzy skidded down onto her lap again, crying *wheee!* He offered up his belly for a rub—Cinnabun's Cuteness Lesson Number Three. With another giggle, Abby obliged.

"You're the sweetest," she cooed.

Fuzzy raced around and repeated his actions. This time, the girl said "Whee!" right along with him as he slid down.

Mrs. Krumpton sent them a look. "Sweetie, could you keep it down? I'm trying to work."

Taking advantage of her attention, Fuzzy swiveled

around in Abby's lap and gave her mother the full force of his Bambi Eyes. *That should do it*, he thought.

Frowning, Mrs. Krumpton asked, "Is something wrong with that creature? It's staring at me very strangely."

Fuzzy sighed.

As she bent over to watch him, Abby's pigtails swung back and forth. "Fuzzy's so adorable," she said. "Don't you just love him?"

From the expression on Mrs. Krumpton's face, love was the last thing she was feeling. Fuzzy himself hadn't looked that crabby since he'd mistaken a green chili for a cucumber and had to face the consequences.

With a sniff, the woman returned to her work. Fuzzy collapsed on Abby's lap. It would take some kind of miracle to win her mother's heart, and he was fresh out of miracles.

Late that night, Fuzzy jolted awake. Abby's room was dark but for a blue nightlight. Had something jostled his cage?

A whiff of flowers assaulted his nostrils, and a shadowy shape bent over the top of the carrier.

"Whoa!"

Suddenly, the portable cage lifted into the air. Fuzzy found his temporary home swaying through one room and another, finally ending up in the brightly lit kitchen. The carrier plunked down on a table.

Mrs. Krumpton's grumpy, late-night face loomed over the cage's opening. "Now then, Mr. Piggie," said Abby's mom. "You and I are going to settle things once and for all."

CHAPTER 15

Survivor: Suburbia

Fuzzy peered up at the PTA president. She glared down at him. In the harsh kitchen light, he noticed the flecks of leftover lipstick clinging to her lips, the faint lines bracketing her mouth, the blue eyes icier than an Arctic river.

He did his best to look friendly. Taking a chance, Fuzzy busted out one of Cinnabun's other cuteness moves, the Adorable Yawn.

"Pets." Mrs. Krumpton sniffed. "You're nothing but trouble."

Fuzzy frowned. He'd already tried Bambi Eyes, the

Belly Roll, and the yawn. He was running out of charming tricks.

"You worm your way into little kids' lives, and when you die, you leave them brokenhearted," said the PTA president. "But does anyone consider that before getting a pet? Never."

Fuzzy shook himself. How'd they get on the subject of death? Humans were a mystery. He gazed up at the woman with his sweetest expression, hoping she'd keep talking and give him something he could use to convince her.

Planting her elbows on the table, Mrs. Krumpton rested her chin on her fists. "It's irresponsible to let kids bond with pets. If we were meant to have animals around us, we'd still be living in the forest."

Having never lived in a forest himself, Fuzzy had no comment. He scratched himself vigorously with a hind leg.

The woman leaned closer, and her nostrils flared like twin train tunnels. Fuzzy shied away. "Don't you dare let my daughter get attached to you," said Mrs. Krumpton. "I won't have her getting her heart broken because of you."

"That's ridiculous," huffed Fuzzy, even though he knew she couldn't understand him. Forming a bond with students was the whole purpose of being a class pet. Sure, it was bittersweet when his kids eventually moved on to the next grade, but pets don't live in the future, they live in the here and now.

Mrs. Krumpton's eyes narrowed. "I'm wise to your game, mister. And I won't let that happen to my Abby."

"What game?" Fuzzy occasionally played hopscotch with the other pets, but he couldn't understand why the woman wouldn't want Abby to enjoy it.

"In fact . . ." Mrs. Krumpton's face took on a sly expression.

Uh-oh. That didn't look promising.

Two hands dove down into the carrier and grabbed him. This wasn't a gentle grip—no, Mrs. Krumpton held him like she was squeezing a toothpaste tube.

Urk! Suddenly, it was hard to breathe.

Up, up Fuzzy rose, until he and Abby's mother were eye to eye.

"Why didn't I think of this sooner?" The woman inspected him as if Fuzzy were something the dog had horked up on the rug. "Of course. Eliminate the pet, eliminate the problem."

Fuzzy's eyes went wide. Holy haystacks! Was Mrs. Krumpton planning what he thought she was planning?

As she carried him across the room, Fuzzy began to wriggle. A little shriek escaped his lips, and Mrs. Krumpton's hands tightened around him. In three strides, they had reached the back door.

The woman shifted one hand off Fuzzy to open it. A cold gust of air chilled him like standing over an open grave.

"Help!" he squealed. But so tightly did she grip him that his cry could barely be heard.

Mrs. Krumpton leered down at Fuzzy. "She'll think you escaped," she said. "She'll be sad, but she'll get over it quickly. Not nearly as bad as if you'd stuck around."

Planting one foot outside the door, Abby's mother bent low and . . . pitched Fuzzy out into the darkness!

"Aaaahh!" His legs scrabbled frantically, grabbing nothing but air. A wave of nausea slid through his gut as he tumbled into the blackness.

Whump! Fuzzy landed heavily in some low, scraggly bushes. By the time he'd freed himself, the back door shut with a solid *shoonk*.

"Hey, wait!" he cried. But Abby's mother had gone. The kitchen light winked out, the locks clicked, and Fuzzy found himself all alone in the great outdoors.

Wiggling whiskers!

Although he liked to think of himself as an Adventure Rodent, Fuzzy preferred to choose his own adventures. He sure wouldn't pick this one. Alone, scared, and out in the cold, with who knew what kind of critters prowling through the night around him?

At that thought, Fuzzy crouched, checking his surroundings. Had he heard some leaves crinkle? Was that a predator's footfall?

Holding as still as a stopped clock, he scanned the darkness with just his eyes. Fuzzy could see next to nothing, but the night was alive with sounds. A creepy birdcall. The yowl of a neighbor's cat. Branches groaning in the breeze.

Everything seemed to warn of a fresh danger.

What to do?

Keeping low, Fuzzy darted for the shelter of the house. The door was locked tight. And he couldn't reach the knob, even if it wasn't.

Silver light from a crescent moon showed no cat door or convenient way back inside, so Fuzzy trudged along the wall, one eye out for danger, one eye out for shelter.

A twig cracked like a gunshot. Fuzzy cringed. He stared and stared, but nothing emerged from the darkness. At long last, he forged onward.

Rounding the corner, Fuzzy gazed up at the windows above. One of these must be Abby's room. But which one?

He wanted to call out to her, but Fuzzy didn't want any predators to hear. If he could somehow climb up to a windowsill, he could peek inside and look for Abby.

Yeah, right. Easier said than done.

It was much too high to jump, even if guinea pigs were jumpers, which they weren't. He glanced left and right. No helpful trees or bushes offered a pathway up.

Fuzzy hugged the wall, continuing on around the house. One window in particular seemed to have a bluish glow, just like Abby's nightlight. Was this her room?

"Psst!" hissed Fuzzy. But the window was closed; she couldn't hear him. He risked a quiet "Hey!" No reaction. If only Fuzzy could tap on her window . . .

He stumbled over a small rock underfoot, and then it hit him:

Pebbles!

He could throw pebbles at her window until Abby woke up and saw him, just like people did in those romantic movies Miss Wills loved. Scooping up a pawful, he took a few steps back, cocked his arm, and threw.

Dink. The pebble plunked harmlessly against the wall, far below his target.

Fuzzy reared back and flung another one. Again it fell short.

Cupping his last pebble in his paw, Fuzzy wound up like a champion baseball pitcher and hurled it with all his might.

Plink. It still landed more than a foot short.

"Suffering mange mites!" he swore. Fuzzy bent to scoop up more ammunition.

A twig cracked behind him. "Having trouble, mate?" asked a raspy voice.

CHAPTER 16

Rocky Raccoon

Fuzzy whirled. A huge, furry shape loomed over him in the darkness. The moonlight revealed a thick body, a triangular head, and the glint of two ebony eyes in a black mask. This was either a robber or a raccoon. Possibly both.

"H-hi," said Fuzzy. "Nice night."

"Peachy," said the masked bandit.

"W-what brings you here?"

The raccoon spread his arms and grinned. "Same as always, mate. Hunting for dinner." He glanced down at Fuzzy's paws. "You know, if you wanna hurt that house, you'll need a bigger rock."

"Oh, uh . . ." Fuzzy didn't know whether to drop the pebbles or fling them at the raccoon. He decided to hang on to them. "No, I was, um, trying to wake up someone in that room."

The burly creature cocked his head, checking out the window. "Need a boost?" he said.

"Beg your pardon?"

"You know, a lift." The raccoon pointed at the window. "If you stood on my shoulders, I reckon you just might be able to reach that sill." He licked his lips.

Fuzzy took a step back. Something about the raccoon's friendly smile seemed a bit . . . hungry.

"No, that's okay," he said.

"No worries," said the masked bandit, rubbing his paws over each other in a washing gesture. "Always happy to help a fellow creature in need." His canine teeth sparkled when he smiled, like sunlight glinting off a pair of daggers.

Taking another step back, Fuzzy bumped into the wall. He wondered what kind of things appeared on a raccoon's dinner menu. Did it include small rodents?

"I—I've changed my mind," said Fuzzy. "Maybe I shouldn't wake up my friend so late."

"Rubbish." The raccoon's grin widened as he cupped his front paws into a stirrup and bent over Fuzzy, blocking out the moon. "Step right here, mate, and all your troubles will be over."

"You're too kind."

Like a Sherman tank of stenchiness, the rank, musky odor of the predator rolled over Fuzzy. His eyes watered. All his senses screamed *danger*.

Two black eyes bored into his, willing Fuzzy to take that final step.

Instead, he flung his pawful of pebbles directly into those eyes—and this time, he hit his target.

"Bugger!" yowled the raccoon, clapping his paws over his eyes.

That was all the opening Fuzzy needed. He bolted, making straight for the nearest bush.

"Get your bum back here!" roared the burly bandit.

Fuzzy risked a glance behind him. The raccoon stumbled in pursuit, still rubbing his eyes.

Reaching the shelter of the shrub, Fuzzy dove beneath it. He got a rude surprise.

Ouch! Sharp spines pierced his back and shoulders, and a cedar-y scent enveloped him. Of all the places he could've taken shelter—a thornbush!

A glance over his shoulder revealed the raccoon rapidly closing in. No time to find a better hiding place. With many an *ooch!* and *owie!* Fuzzy wriggled deeper into the heart of the bush.

Ka-crackle. The raccoon plunged into the shrub, reaching for Fuzzy.

"Blistering barnacles!" he cried, reeling backward and shaking his paws. "That hurts!"

"It's supposed to," said Fuzzy.

"Get your carcass out here."

"Gee, let me think about that," said Fuzzy, pretending to consider. "Um, I'll have to go with *no way!*"

The raccoon growled. "You are the stubbornest, rudest, most unhelpful dinner I've ever met."

"That's because I'm not your—*ow!*—dinner," said Fuzzy, unhooking himself from a thorn. "I'm Fuzzy."

"We'll see about that!" snarled the raccoon.

Once more, the burly predator lunged into the bush, paws grasping. "Frigga fragga foo!" he swore, backing away. The raccoon pulled out a couple of thorns with his teeth and popped his wounded paw into his mouth.

"Serves you right for trying to eat people," said Fuzzy. Somehow, he felt braver inside the prickly bush.

"*Uff*, it's the law of the, *mmf*, jungle," said the raccoon around the paw in his mouth.

"Not *my* law," said Fuzzy. "I'm no Jungle Rodent; I'm a City Rodent."

The raccoon shot him a glare hot enough to burn a polar bear's butt. "You're in for it, boyo. Come on out of there, *pronto*."

"Nope. Think I'll make a summer home in this bush." Fuzzy tried for a luxurious stretch and pricked himself on a thorn. "I could—*ow!*—stay here all month."

"You wouldn't."

"I might," said Fuzzy. "Why don't you go pick on a defenseless trash can or something?"

"Maybe I will, and maybe I won't," said the predator. He shook his wounded paw. "But you'll have to leave sometime for food and water. And when you do— *bam!*—I'll be there."

"Good to know," said Fuzzy. He tried to sound brave, but the thought of being stalked by a hungry raccoon had him trembling.

After a few minutes of pacing up and down outside the bush, the predator gave a disgusted growl and headed off to seek easier prey. Fuzzy didn't budge. All senses alert, he kept watch for the raccoon's return.

Not so much as a whisker showed. An owl hooted. A distant dog barked.

After what felt like ages on high alert, Fuzzy yawned. The excitement had taken its toll. His eyelids drooped, feeling heavier and heavier, until finally he fell into a deep, deep sleep.

"*Fuh*-zzyyyy!"

The distant sound of his name being called roused Fuzzy the next morning. He blinked at the bright sunshine and stretched, only to remember—too late— where he was.

"Yowch!"

Rubbing his leg, Fuzzy scanned the area around the thornbush. No raccoon. No hungry dogs. Nothing but a shaggy backyard garden.

Again, someone called his name. From the sound of it, Abby was searching for him inside the house.

Holy haystacks!

With a jolt, Fuzzy realized that today was Monday. If the girl didn't find him soon, she'd leave for school, and he'd never make his way back to Miss Wills's class. Somehow, he had to catch her attention.

"Ow! Ugh! Yikes!" With many a poke and a prick, Fuzzy wriggled his way out from under the spiny bush. Thorns tore his lovely coat, but he pushed onward.

Breaking free, he dashed around the house as fast as he could. Was he too late? As Fuzzy neared the kitchen door, he could hear voices from inside.

"Looks like he's gone, Abs," said Mrs. Krumpton.

"But poor Fuzzy!" said Abby. "He could be any-where. *Fuh-zzyyy!*"

Wheek! Wheek! Fuzzy bounced up and down, squeak-ing with all his might.

"Did you hear something?" asked Abby. The kitchen doorknob rattled.

"No use looking out there, sweetie," said her mother. "It's a shame, but . . ."

Wheek-wheek-wheek! Fuzzy scratched on the door.

"I definitely heard something," said Abby.

"Don't—" Mrs. Krumpton began.

But the lock clicked open and the doorknob was turning. Fuzzy barely had enough time to lunge aside before the door swung open. There stood Abby, with her mother right behind her.

"Fuzzy!" she cried, bending down to scoop him up. "*There* you are. You scared me! How did you get out? You look like you've had a rough night."

Fuzzy had never been so glad to see anyone in his life. He snuggled the girl, licking her cheek over and over. And then his eyes fell on Mrs. Krumpton's glower. She was *so* not happy to see him.

Her scowl told a story. Fuzzy might have won this round, but the battle was far from over.

CHAPTER 17

A Handy Janitor

At school that day, everyone was twitchier than a long-tailed cat in a rocking chair factory. Before class, Abby collected loads of signatures for her petition. More SAVE OUR PETS signs had sprouted on the walls, and the afterschool meeting was all anyone could talk about.

"Are you coming?" Heavy-Handed Jake asked Malik.

"You bet," said the boy. "Abby and I are going to deliver our petitions and testify."

"That's right," said Abby, full of fire. "We're even making a special poster—nice and big, so everyone can see."

As Fuzzy listened to his students put their heads together, he realized something. Many of the kids, parents, and teachers would attend that meeting, but not the ones most affected: the pets.

While focusing on changing Mrs. Flake's and Mrs. Krumpton's minds, Fuzzy and his friends had forgotten to figure out how to attend the meeting themselves. They'd hoped the charm offensive would cancel it.

But that hadn't happened. And now, unless they came up with something quick, the pets would miss the meeting that would decide their fate.

That just wouldn't do.

All through morning lessons, Fuzzy champed at the bit. Did he dare try contacting the other pets during lunch when all the kids were away? It'd be risky. Suppose someone caught him roaming around outside his habitat? Then what?

Fuzzy finally decided it was a gamble he had to make.

When lunchtime came, he waited until the kids and teacher left for the cafeteria.

And waited.

And *waited*.

Although everyone else had taken off, two students stubbornly refused to go. Malik and Abby sat together, eating their sack lunches and discussing their presentation.

Fuzzy fidgeted, looking back and forth between the kids and the clock. On the one hand, he was glad they were so enthusiastic about saving classroom pets. On the other hand, he wished they'd take their enthusiasm outside, so he could go meet with his friends.

But they didn't leave. As soon as they finished their lunches, Abby and Malik collected a folder, some glue, markers, scissors, and a large poster board. They brought all the items over to the worktable.

Nearly half of lunchtime had slipped by. How long would these kids take? Fuzzy wondered.

Chatting as they worked, Abby and Malik cut out images of Fuzzy and the other pets and arranged them on the poster board. After some discussion about the layout, they pasted the photos in place, carefully adding each pet's name.

"I want them to see who we're talking about," said Abby. "Not just *pets*, but Fuzzy and Cinnabun and Sassafras."

"I like that," said Malik. "More personal."

Fuzzy admired their dedication. But he really wished they would hurry. Now only ten minutes remained before class started. If the kids left *right now*, he just might be able to visit Vinnie in 4-B and make it back in time.

But they still didn't leave. Instead, Malik and Abby carefully lettered slogans onto the poster board in electric blue and lipstick red. They practiced what they were going to say and stapled together their petitions.

The bell rang. Soon, kids flowed back into the room.

Fuzzy sighed, deflated. So much for that plan. If he wanted to attend the meeting, he'd have to figure out how to get there on his own.

The afternoon passed in a blur, like the world as seen from a Tilt-A-Whirl. (Not one of Fuzzy's favorite experiences with a pet-sitter.) As the final bell rang, Miss Wills asked the students to linger for a moment or two.

"I hope that many of you are coming to this meeting to support class pets," she said.

A cheer rose from the group.

"I'm glad," she continued. "And I want you to know that, whichever way this vote turns out—" Here, something seemed to catch in Miss Wills's gullet, and she paused for a moment to regain control. "I—I'm sure Fuzzy has really enjoyed being our class pet."

Fuzzy's eyes got misty. His throat felt tighter than tube socks on a T. rex. Could this really be the end of his time with Room 5-B?

"Fuzzy's the best!" cried Loud Brandon.

The students took up a chant: "Fuz-zy! Fuz-zy! Fuz-zy!" And, still chanting, they trooped out the door. Miss Wills tidied up her desk and papers for a few minutes, and then came over to Fuzzy's cage.

Softly stroking his back, she said, "Don't you worry, big guy. We'll do our very best."

As soon as she left, Fuzzy pushed his platform, blocks, and ball into escape positions. But halfway through climbing them, a thought froze him in his tracks:

Mr. Darius. The custodian always came by to tidy up after school.

If Fuzzy left now, the janitor would find an empty cage.

What to do?

While he wavered, Fuzzy heard a key turning in the lock. The door creaked open, and there stood the man himself, Mr. Darius. But instead of his usual push broom, the custodian carried a good-sized cardboard box.

With long strides, he made his way to Fuzzy's habitat. "Hey, little buddy," he said. "Looks like you're already planning a getaway."

Oops. If guinea pigs could blush, Fuzzy's face would've turned beet red.

"Don't worry," said the man. "I'm not here to bust you; I'm here to help." And with that, he set the box on a nearby table, lifted Fuzzy with both hands, and gently deposited him into the box.

That was surprising enough. But another surprise awaited inside.

"Cinnabun!" cried Fuzzy.

The rabbit looked up from grooming her chest fur. "Afternoon, Brother Fuzzy. Isn't this exciting?"

"But why are you here?" he asked. "And what are we doing in this box?"

Mr. Darius hefted their container and left the room, setting the box down on something in the hallway. It was frustrating not being able to see much, but then Fuzzy heard the familiar *squeak-squeak-squeak*, and he knew they were on the custodian's cart. Above the high sides of the box, the ceiling tiles scrolled by.

Cinnabun smiled. "I do believe Mr. Darius is taking us on a field trip."

"But I wanted to watch the meeting," said Fuzzy.

"You may get your wish," said the rabbit.

"How do you mean?"

A muffled voice came from somewhere nearby. "Is that the Fuzzmeister?" called Luther.

"What's going on?" said Fuzzy.

"We caught a ride with the Darius Taxi Service," the boa replied. "Crazy, baby."

The cart stopped outside another door. And another. Before long, Mr. Darius had collected all the class pets

161

and was wheeling them along the hallway. Judging by the ever-strengthening smell of hot dog buns, chili, and other bygone meals, they were headed for the multipurpose room.

Fuzzy heaved a sigh of relief. They would make the meeting after all.

A babble of voices washed over them as the cart pushed through the double doors. The smell of sweat, perfume, and coffee mingled with the food odors to create a powerful bouquet. From the look of things, Mr. Darius was taking them right up to the front of the room.

"What's all this?" demanded a piercing, nasal voice. Mrs. Krumpton.

By standing on his hind legs, Fuzzy could just see the custodian's expression, calm and unruffled.

"I've brought along everyone who's most affected by this meeting," said Mr. Darius.

Mrs. Krumpton's makeup-coated face loomed over Fuzzy's box, and snarled in disgust when she saw him. "But these aren't people," said the PTA president. "They're animals."

"They're more than that," said the custodian.

"That's right!" squeaked Fuzzy.

The blonde woman folded her arms. "They're nothing but trouble, and I won't have these creatures at my meeting."

The custodian's jaw tightened. He made no move to depart.

"First of all, it's not your meeting, it's *our* meeting," said a familiar voice. Over the box's edge, Fuzzy could just make out the gray-blonde hair of Principal Flake. "And secondly, these pets are part of our Leo Gumpus family. If we're making a decision that concerns them, they should be present."

"But—but this is so irregular," sputtered the PTA president.

"Life is irregular," said Mrs. Flake.

"It'll disrupt everything."

The principal was as calm as a frozen lake in February. "It'll be just fine. I'm sure if the pets get restless, Darius would be happy to settle them down."

"That's right," said the custodian. "But I won't have to. These pets are better behaved than plenty of people I could name."

"Amen, brother," said Cinnabun primly.

Mrs. Krumpton huffed and blustered, but she knew when she was outmaneuvered. Her face disappeared from view, and a few seconds later, Fuzzy heard her amplified voice. "People, if you could all take your seats. We're about to start the meeting."

Fuzzy felt his box rise into the air and settle onto a hard surface. Then, it very slowly tilted until it was on its side. Moving with it, he and Cinnabun carefully stepped to the mouth of the box and looked out.

Fuzzy gasped.

They sat at the very edge of the stage, gazing into a room full of humans on folding chairs. A ripple of unease sloshed through Fuzzy's belly at the sight of all those faces. The audience murmured as Mr. Darius set the other boxes onstage and tipped them sideways, so that all the pets could watch the proceedings.

Fuzzy thought Mr. Darius must be the kindest human around. Or at least tied with Miss Wills.

"Ladies and gentlemen, boys and girls," said Principal Flake over the microphone. "Thank you all for coming. Let's begin."

Fuzzy bit his lip. Cinnabun blinked rapidly and fidgeted.

"Are you ready?" she asked.

"Not even a little bit," he said. "But here goes nothing."

CHAPTER 18

Five Reasons Why

From their vantage point, Fuzzy and Cinnabun couldn't see the other pets in their boxes, but they had a ringside view of the audience, the bigwigs' table in front of it, and the backs of the bigwigs' heads. Besides Mrs. Krumpton and Principal Flake, Fuzzy recognized a teacher, Mr. Chopra. Two humans he'd seen around school also shared the table. Fuzzy figured them for PTA members.

Taking charge of the meeting, the principal laid out the rules.

"First, our PTA president, Krissy Krumpton, will explain her proposal," said Mrs. Flake. "We will let some people speak, both for and against, and then we'll all vote on the matter. Mrs. Krumpton, if you would begin?"

The PTA president cleared her throat and tossed back her long blonde hair. That golden sheaf reminded Fuzzy of hay. But he knew that nothing she said would be nearly as nice as his favorite food. He felt a twinge of regret sharper than a double-edged sword that he had failed to charm her.

"For too long, we have lived with danger in our midst," Mrs. Krumpton began. "An unseen danger that threatens all our children."

"Yeah," said Igor's voice from the box beside them. "Rat farts."

"Hush, Brother Igor," said Cinnabun.

From the other side, Vinnie's voice chimed in. "Yeah, I can hear ya, Dinosaur Breath."

"Shhh!" The rabbit shushed him.

Mrs. Krumpton leaned into her microphone. "Don't let their innocent looks fool you. Animals present a very real danger to our children. They can bite—"

"I'd like to bite *her*," said Igor.

"They carry diseases," Mrs. Krumpton continued.

"For the last time, rats are clean animals!" cried Vinnie.

"And kids can be allergic to them without knowing until it's too late. But worst of all, they don't live very long."

Fuzzy shook his head. This woman had death on the brain.

"Compared to what?" said Cinnabun. "We live a lot longer than doodlebugs."

Mrs. Krumpton's shoulders stiffened under her cascade of golden hair. "Is it fair to our children to let

them get attached to something that will die so quickly? Some say it's better to have loved and lost than to never have loved at all. I say skip the heartbreak. Protect our children from this loss. Ban all classroom pets."

"Geez Louise," said Vinnie. "What's her deal?"

"That woman is lower than a snake's belly in a wagon rut," huffed Cinnabun. "No offense, Brother Luther."

"None taken, Missy Mi*sss*," said the boa.

Murmurs erupted in the audience. Some folks were nodding, but many were frowning or shaking their heads. It looked to Fuzzy like the group was pretty evenly split.

"Thank you for your proposal, Mrs. Krumpton," said Principal Flake, though her tone sounded anything but grateful. "We will now open up the floor for anyone to express their opinions on the matter."

"Anyone?" said Mrs. Krumpton. "I think we should limit comments to ten people or fewer. Otherwise we'll be here through dinnertime, and no one wants that."

Mrs. Flake disagreed. But when the head table voted on the matter, it came out three to two in favor of a shorter session.

"Very well," said the principal. "Everyone, please keep your comments brief and respectful. Who's first?"

Hands shot up like prickles on a porcupine. To start, the principal called on Malik's mother, who was sitting in the first row with her son. Mrs. Summers stood in place, half-turning to address both the audience and the head table. She smoothed down her skirt front.

"Like many of you, I never used to object to the idea of pets in the classroom," she said. "Until a week ago, when a class pet got my son into a terrible accident."

Fuzzy heard some sharp inhalations from the crowd, but many people still looked skeptical.

"He brought the class guinea pig home for the weekend," Mrs. Summers continued. "Malik let the creature out of its cage while he was rehearsing a scene for a play."

Cinnabun shot Fuzzy a glance. He hung his head, unable to meet her eyes.

"At a crucial moment, this animal got in the way," said Malik's mother. "My son was hit in the head. He could have developed brain damage or even died."

From his chair beside her, Malik started to rise. "I'm totally fine, Mom!"

"Only through blind luck," said Mrs. Summers, pushing him back down into his seat. "I'm with Krissy; we should ban all classroom pets."

Cinnabun touched Fuzzy's shoulder. "Luther told me all about it."

"I'm so sorry," he said. "I was just trying to help."

She didn't accuse him; she didn't even have to. "Oh, Fuzzy." The note of gentle reproach in her voice made him want to shrivel up and disappear.

When Mrs. Summers sat down, the school nurse, Mr. Wong, rose to speak. "There's been a lot of loose talk about pets carrying diseases," he said, "and I want to set the record straight."

"About time," came Vinnie's muffled voice.

Mr. Wong raked back his hair with one hand. "I worked for five years in a vet's office, and during that time, our clients didn't report even one case of a pet passing on a disease to a human."

"See?" said Vinnie. "Told ya so."

"The truth is," the nurse continued, "practicing good personal hygiene and keeping pets healthy and vaccinated—which we do—completely minimizes any risk. Come on, people. These are pets, not rats with bubonic plague."

"Hey!" Vinnie objected. "That's stereotyping."

After answering a couple of questions from Mrs. Krumpton and Principal Flake, Mr. Wong sat back down. The next parent to testify went on and on about the dangers of rabies. *Clearly*, thought Fuzzy, *someone hasn't been listening to the nurse.*

Then a third-grade boy made an emotional appeal, saying that Mistletoe the mouse was one of his best friends, and that people shouldn't be allowed to take away your friends. His classmates cheered him on.

"You tell 'em, Ethan!" squeaked Mistletoe from Vinnie's box.

A couple more parents spoke, and a couple more

kids. After Miss Wills had her turn, Mrs. Krumpton wanted to hold the vote right then and there. But the principal called for one last speaker.

Abby's arm was flailing like windshield wipers in a hurricane, so Mrs. Flake picked her. Blushing but determined, the girl grabbed her poster and made her way to the front of the room.

Mrs. Krumpton leaned forward urgently. "Sweetie?" she said in a low voice, covering the microphone. "You don't need to testify. Mommy's got this."

"She wants to speak," said Mrs. Flake.

Abby gave the principal a grateful nod. Wordlessly, Malik rose to join her, ignoring his mother's pointed look. He set their petitions on the head table.

"Here's two hundred and forty-three signatures in favor of keeping our pets," he said. Malik stood beside Abby, cutting his eyes to her.

The girl cleared her throat loudly and ducked her head. Abby seemed daunted by all the attention from the audience. *She's probably never had this many people who want to listen to her before,* thought Fuzzy. Malik nudged Abby's shoulder in an encouraging way.

"Um, Miss Wills always tells us that we live in a democracy," said Abby at last. "She says that everyone has the right to express their opinion. That we should speak up when we see injustice."

From an aisle seat, Miss Wills smiled, giving her a thumbs-up.

"So Malik and I did an extra-credit report on why we need class pets like these," said Abby. She turned to look at Fuzzy, Cinnabun, and the others.

"Aww," said Cinnabun. "I like her."

"Now, Abigail," said Mrs. Krumpton. "You really don't know—"

"Let her speak," said Principal Flake in a stern, *I'm the principal here* tone. The PTA president stiffened, but she held her tongue.

Abby's gaze flicked uncertainly over the two women. Then she turned back to the audience. "Um, so here are our top five reasons why we need to keep our classroom pets. Reason Number Five: Taking care of pets encourages a sense of responsibility."

"Tell that to Jamaica, who forgot to change my water," said Igor from the next box over.

"Shh!" Fuzzy and Cinnabun shushed him.

"Reason Number Four," said Malik. "Kids who don't feel as confident in their reading abilities feel safer reading aloud to a pet."

"He's right!" shouted Loud Brandon. He grimaced when he realized what he'd just revealed about himself. "Oops."

The audience chuckled.

"Reason Number Three," said Abby in a stronger voice. "Cuddles."

"Huh?" said a dad in the front row. "I don't get it."

Abby addressed the kids in the audience. "School can be stressful, right, guys?"

Kids shouted things like, "You know it!" "Ugh, standardized tests!" and "Oral reports are the worst!"

She bobbed her head in agreement. "We found studies that said when students can cuddle pets, it lowers their stress and anxiety levels."

Vinnie's cackle reached Fuzzy from the next box over. "Well, that leaves you out, Spiky Boy," he called to Igor. "Yer the least cuddly creature on the planet."

"Zip it, Plague Breath," the iguana retorted.

"Reason Number Two," said Malik. "When you help take care of a pet, you learn empathy and have more respect for animals."

Cinnabun beamed. "Respect's a good thing."

Thinking about everything they'd been through, Fuzzy said, "And we could all use a little more empathy."

"But this weekend I learned the number-one reason of all." Abby glanced back at Fuzzy, and he felt a warm flutter in his chest. "And that's love."

"That's ridiculous." Mrs. Krumpton snorted. "Abby, sit down right—"

Before the principal could intervene, Abby burst out, "No, Mom!"

Her mother rocked back in her seat. "*What* did you say?"

"It's my turn to speak." Abby's lip quivered. Her face was pale but determined. "You never listen to me, but this time I'm going to finish."

"Let the girl speak!" shouted someone from the crowd.

"Yeah!" cried another parent.

Mrs. Krumpton sputtered indignantly.

One of the PTA members at the table reached over and laid a hand on the blonde woman's arm, making a calming gesture with her other hand.

"This weekend," said Abby, "I had a terrible time at my soccer game. I was sad; I felt bad about myself." She looked at the floor. "But when I spent time cuddling with Fuzzy afterward . . ."

Fuzzy swallowed a lump in his throat.

"His love made me feel better," said the girl. "I know that's not scientific, and I didn't read it in a study, but it's true. Pets love us, and we love them right back." Abby cleared her throat. "And if that's not enough of a reason to keep them around, I don't know what is."

"But," said Mrs. Krumpton, her voice thick with emotion. "But what if they die and leave you alone? Like Fifi."

The look Abby turned on her mom was a tender one. "Then they die, Mom. But their love stays on."

"Oh, Abby." Choking back a sob, her mother jumped to her feet and wrapped her daughter in a tight hug. They rocked gently back and forth.

"Aww," said Cinnabun. She threw an arm around Fuzzy's shoulders. "Now, ain't that sweeter than a sugar boat on a honey sea?"

CHAPTER 19

Doctor Love Triumphs

In the end, the count wasn't even close. The students and parents voted overwhelmingly to keep classroom pets at Leo Gumpus Elementary. A great cheer went up when Principal Flake announced the voting results.

Fuzzy and Cinnabun joined paws and whooped for joy. Unable to contain himself, Fuzzy began popcorning with a *wheek wheek wheek!*—until he bonked his head on the box's top. After that, he settled for mellower cheering.

The rabbit glowed with happiness. "Well, hush my mouth, Brother Fuzzy. I don't know what to say."

"Congratulations to us?" said Fuzzy.

She shook her head wonderingly. "You got us into this whole mess by acting on your impulses."

Fuzzy held up a paw. "I said I'm sorry."

"But you also got us *out* of this mess by acting on your impulses."

Fuzzy turned up his palms. "I'm funny that way. But the kids come first."

"First and always," agreed Cinnabun.

Something thumped on the box to their left. "Way to go, Chubby Cheeks!" cried Vinnie. "Or should I say, Doctor Love?"

Cinnabun giggled. Fuzzy's face felt warm.

"Does this mean the club isn't going to kick me out?" he asked.

Patting his shoulder, Cinnabun said, "I don't see how we could when the school just voted for you to stay. You're safe . . . for now," she added teasingly.

Fuzzy looked up to see kids crowding around the pets' boxes. Some faces he recognized, some he didn't, but all were grinning and praising the pets.

"Holy macaroni!" Mistletoe squeaked. "It's like we're movie stars!"

"Dream on, Short Stack," said Vinnie, but Fuzzy could hear the affection in his voice.

Then Fuzzy saw someone he knew pushing through the crowd. Abby seemed to have an extra spring in her step, an extra twinkle in her eye. She reached into the box, lifting Fuzzy out for a cuddle. He burrowed into her shoulder, nuzzling.

"Oh, Fuzzy," said Abby. "You're the best."

"Well, maybe second-best," he chirped modestly.

"I couldn't have done this without you. You gave me the courage I needed to stand up and speak."

Fuzzy doubted that very much, but he thought it was sweet of her to say.

After being passed around from student to student for a few minutes, Fuzzy was ready for some peace and quiet. Almost as if sensing this, Mr. Darius appeared. He reclaimed Fuzzy and the others from the kids who'd been petting them, and returned the pets to their boxes.

On the ride back to their classrooms, Fuzzy and Cinnabun shared a comfortable silence. After all the excitement, both felt truly tuckered out.

At Room 5-B, the custodian carried Fuzzy's box inside and lifted him out of it. Placing him back in his habitat with a last pat and a bit of carrot, Mr. Darius smiled down. "I guess those posters I put up made a difference after all," he said.

"You did that?" said Fuzzy.

Almost as if he understood, the custodian said, "I'm glad they came to their senses before it was too late. In my book, a school without pets just isn't a school."

After Mr. Darius shut the door, Fuzzy treated himself to a long, long nap.

By unspoken agreement, none of the pets showed up at their clubhouse the next day after school. Fuzzy didn't know about the rest of them, but after the stress of the past couple weeks, he felt lazier than a sleepy snail riding piggyback on a sloth. It wasn't until Wednesday afternoon that the group gathered again.

When Fuzzy ambled down the ramp into their hangout, Luther hailed him with, "Hey, Fuzzarooney! The rodent of the hour!"

Vinnie clapped him on the back. "So, what's the good word?"

"You know that girl Abby who testified to keep us at school?" said Fuzzy.

"Our pigtailed angel? What about her?"

Fuzzy grinned. "Today she told the class that her mom is finally letting her have a pet at home!"

"Well, bless my ears and whiskers," said Cinnabun. "That was one persuasive argument."

Luther smirked. "That there's a future lawyer, baby."

"But that's not all the news, folks!" said Sassafras, gliding in for a landing.

"What's up?" asked Mistletoe.

The parakeet hopped around, ruffling the feathers on her head. "I heard Mrs. Martinez talking to the principal today. Mrs. Flake told her that Abby's argument was almost *too* persuasive."

"How's that?" asked Fuzzy.

Sassafras cackled. "Not one, not two, but *four* other classrooms are talking about getting pets."

Cinnabun's nose twitched. "You mean . . . ?"

"We'll have to get a bigger clubhouse," said Sassafras. "Turns out, everyone loves pets!"

A smile spread across Fuzzy's face as the others whooped it up. *Of course everybody loves pets,* he thought, *because pets love everybody.*